for Virginia
from Abigail
Xmas 88

Janice — I'm passing
this on to you it's
a delightful little
story I'm sure
you'll enjoy..
Merry Christmas
1997
Love, the Adams

COURTING
EMMA
HOWE

Also by Margaret A. Robinson
Arrivals & Departures

COURTING
EMMA
HOWE

A NOVEL

Margaret A. Robinson

ADLER&ADLER

Published in the United States in 1987 by
Adler & Adler, Publishers, Inc.
4550 Montgomery Avenue
Bethesda, Maryland 20814

Printed in the United States of America

In a slightly different version, the first two chapters of
this novel appeared as the short story, "Proposal," in
The Pennsylvania Review, the University of Pittsburgh,
fall/winter 1986.

for Claude

A writer is upheld by many hands. I would
like to thank Pat Hale, Gail Hochman, Ruth Malone,
Lil Patterson, Betsy Sachs, and Elizabeth Winthrop
for sticking by me through this book.

COURTING

EMMA

HOWE

I

ARTHUR SMOLLET, in work clothes, a shaggy moustache concealing his mouth, sat at the table in his bedroom, writing to Emma Howe. Nothing special about the letter, he thought. Just staying in touch. He dipped his pen:

North Falls, Wash.
December 27, 1904

My dear friend Emma,
I hope you spent a pleasant Christmas, as I did, with plenty of friends and family around you. I passed the day with my near-est neighbors, the Browns. We had turkey, and carol singing, and the mince pies were fine.
The winter rains keep coming, he went on in his small almost too neat handwriting, *but I'm making headway. With any luck, the new clearing I'm working on will be ready for stump pull-ing soon.*

Through the window, he gave a couple of trees an even, adversarial look. He'd been at work that day on the new area with axe and saw and he could feel that work in his back. He was a small man—sinewy rather than brawny, persistent rather than unusually strong. He had turned thirty-five a few weeks earlier, and the birthday had made him feel time breathing down his neck. His own father had died before the age of forty.

He was sick of the winter rains, eager for spring, and thought how the first signs would be along soon.

You'd admire the ferns here, he wrote, *which will be poking*

1

up before long. They grow waist high—the wetness seems to suit them. I'm glad it suits something, for I'm tired of it though I'm drier now with the new wood floor in both rooms.

He had doubled the space of his original cabin when he built this new room. His writing table and a bookshelf made it an office. His clothes, hung on pegs, and the bed, covered with a quilt that came with him on a freighter around the Horn, made it a bedroom as well.

As a sailor on shore leave at home, he had read in the newspaper that the government was giving away small tracts of land in "areas dangerous or difficult to settle." He decided to try his hand at homesteading; he had always wanted to own his own land. So eager was he for the government parcel (the deed that he later received bore the signature of President McKinley himself) that he signed for it sight unseen back in Somerville, Massachusetts. Months later, after he had sailed down one side of South America and up the other to claim it, he discovered he'd been made the owner of—in exchange for a promise to clear it—a piece of land that back home would have been called a swamp. Or almost a swamp. A wet, overgrown jungle.

There was nothing for it but to get to work. He took a job at a lumber camp to keep himself and learn what he needed to know. Later he hired out at the sawmill, on the road gang, on other ranches in the area, always clearing his own land in his extra hours. He cut his own trails, packed supplies in on his back, built his cabin, now the main room of his house. Seven years after his first disheartening sight of it, when he crashed through the rank underbrush with surveyor's tools, the jungle was at last supporting him as a working farm.

The room was dark and he was hungry. Light flowered out of the lamp in the other room as he struck a match and lighted it. He added wood to the stove; the fire was smoking. Martin Vogel, Arthur's hired hand, must have taken sticks for the noon fire from the new pile, where the wood was both green and wet. There was no such thing as *dry* in this narrow valley. He had drained the brown watery network that pooled and dribbled over much of his property, creating Smollett Creek. It flowed into a pond three-quarters of a mile away, on the parcel belonging to his neighbors, the Browns. But no labor of man's could stop the water falling from the sky. Despite the many winters he'd endured Puget Sound weather (his ranch was thirty-five miles northeast of Seattle), he was still not used to the wet. It was like living in the bottom of a cup.

He found corn bread and a pan of leftover stew in his food safe. He filled his kettle and put it and stew on the stove to heat. Then, with a little nervous jump in his stomach, which he felt even though there wasn't a soul around for miles to spy on him, he took the pile of Emma's letters from the drawer in his writing table in the other room. The most recent one, her Christmas letter, contained her photograph. He sat down to warm his feet on the stove and study it.

Emma was rather stiffly posed on a lawn, a croquet mallet in her hand, a ball and hoop close to the edge of her skirt. She'd written that she was twenty-five. He thought her body looked younger than that, and her face older. She had made a point of telling him she was a Methodist. She was also a member of the Grange. She wore no hat. Her hair was swept up from her face and piled on top of her head the way women wore their hair after they stopped braiding it and before they started putting it in a bun behind. He liked her eyes, which were large and luminous, but she didn't look happy and he guessed that she disliked being photographed.

She made a spare, angular figure in her plain plaid dress, her head tilted diffidently and her lips painfully shut over what must be—any fool could tell—extremely buck teeth. She had written to him early on that she was "no beauty." Their correspondence started when he responded to her poem about bloodroot in the "Contributor's Corner" of the magazine *Nature's Friends*. (*"Dear Miss Howe,"* he'd written, *"You should see the bloodroot out here. The blooms are as big as teacups."*) When she said she was "no beauty," he'd thought she was being falsely modest. Women did that sort of thing, ran themselves down so a man would be forced to praise them all the more. But Emma was, in fact, homely. She was shy and horse-faced, the kind of woman most men laugh at or ignore.

But he liked her. Her picture, when it came, didn't put him off. He remembered that as a small boy he had believed his mother's face to be the most beautiful in the world. He was

3

shocked to learn, at about the age of six, that the world didn't agree with him—by any objective standard, his mother's features were completely ordinary. About the same time, his mother's concern for him changed, in his view, from loving sweetness to a clinging need to monitor his every act. He remembered her holding him on her lap like a baby and his fighting to get *down*. She tightened her grip. He wriggled and fought. Her voice and arms embraced him tighter. Finally he had kicked free.

He prided himself on looking beyond appearances, and in Emma's letters he had seen sympathy and wit. What really drew him to her had nothing to do with looks. It was her description in her Christmas letter of harvesting a cabbage she had grown from seed, slicing it in half, and standing in awe of the shapes revealed by her knife: *"Each half had a white trunk, pale green curving branches, and a crown of dark green leaves like a tree,"* she'd written. *"If I were an artist, I'd paint cut cabbages. I hope that does not seem odd to you."*

It hadn't seemed odd to him. For half an hour, it had made him love her.

He poured coffee and sat down to his dinner. As he bit into the coarse, gritty corn bread, he remembered his mother's johnnycake, high, light, and tender, still steaming when cut and the palest yellow. The butter, slathered on with a wooden paddle from the crock, soaked into every crumb. He wondered if Emma could cook.

Wiping his fingers on his pants, he fetched the pen and letter from the other room and placed them beside his meal. He added a sentence, softening his boast about his new floors: *But I am a poor hand at baking. My corn bread could easily drive a nail.* He knocked the chunk, minus one bite, against the edge of his plate, *tunk, tunk.* It was as solid as hardtack. He soaked the bitten place for a minute in his stew before he gnawed off another mouthful.

Amos Brill, the preacher at the Methodist church, a man with a ginger-colored beard and rheumy eyes, had been after Arthur to marry. Last Sunday afternoon he had come to call.

"You need a woman to do for you, Mr. Smollett," the preacher had said. "The Lord meant for us to go through life in pairs.

'Two by two' the Noah story says. Marriage is a holy estate. Besides, as you know, the town could use more women."

"Town!" Arthur had thought. Leave it to a busy-body preacher to convert the general store, which doubled as the post office, the Odd Fellows' Hall, and the one-room Methodist church into a "town." Well, there were the station, the school, the finishing mill, and a handful of houses. But even "village" overstated the case. "Settlement" was more like it.

"I do for myself pretty well," he'd replied, and served the preacher tea in clean cups. He was proud of the clearing he had made in the rotting tangle of deadwood logs and undergrowth, of the sunlight he had brought into the valley by felling the trees. In the spring, he'd enlarge his gardens, to meet the demand for vegetables in the logging camps.

He enjoyed his correspondence with Emma. She wrote a good letter and had a sweet nature *("I admire your accomplishments,"* she'd told him. *"You seem, in all you set your hand to, to show a true, manly, and independent spirit.")* But he was content to leave it at that. At first they wrote about wild flowers, comparing those in North Falls to those in Warwick, Vermont. Then they wrote about their families and themselves. Emma seemed a great favorite with the neighborhood children. But as the oldest daughter and the "home" girl (her two younger and presumably prettier sisters were married and gone), she was saddled with the care of two difficult aunts. One had fits; the other had spells. Of his family, Arthur had written to Emma, *"My father, whom I loved in spite of his weakness, is dead. Of my mother, I can summon up few truly pleasant memories except that she had a light hand with biscuits."*

Amos Brill wasn't the only one who had been nudging Arthur. Harry Snow, who presided plumply at the general store, had been dropping hints as well. "Goin'ta put your head in the halter one of these days?" Harry had asked last Saturday night, when Arthur stopped in as usual for supplies.

"Not likely," Arthur had replied.

Harry had given a hitch to his pants, trying in vain to make them keep company with his vest. "You been getting a steady stream of mail from Vermont."

"Harry," Arthur had said. "I've just gotten my life trued up.

5

I'm not looking to skew it. The trouble with you married men is you want company in your misery." That answer, Arthur had thought, put Harry in his place.

Finished eating now, Arthur rinsed his dishes in hot water from the kettle and then sat again by the stove to complete his letter:

Sunday last was a day of rare event—I had a visitor, the preacher, who paid a call. He's a meddlesome person—I hate to be interfered with in any way—but our conversation was polite enough. My tidy housekeeping surprised him some, I think. As if a bachelor couldn't fend for himself but must live like a bear in a cave. As a youth, I felt cramped working in my father's hardware store and was pleased when the doctor ordered me to sea as a remedy for my asthma. My term as a seaman cured the asthma, but left me still to take orders and salute, to fetch and carry. Now at last I own land and a house and do work of my own choosing. As my friend who wishes for my happiness, I know you will rejoice, my dear Emma, when I tell you that I finally have a whole, complete, and satisfying life. The only thing I want is a little less rain!

He wished her a Happy New Year, briskly signed his name, and then, heeding a call of nature, took the lamp and followed the path to the outhouse, built with a waist-high door to prevent gases from collecting and possibly exploding. He slipped off his suspenders, unbuttoned his pants, and sat. The fullness of his bowels was pleasurable, and the release of them even more so. The rain had let up—just a light sprinkle now and again. He sat a minute, thinking of nothing in particular, gazing at the droplets gathering like silver beads along the edge of the roof.

The swatch of newspaper he tore off for wiping contained an article about a new Luther Burbank hybrid ("an everlasting Australian flower with a large pink blossom that does not shed") next to an advertisement for the laxative Fletcher's Castoria. He heaved an involuntary sigh. For years his mother had come at him with a bottle and a spoon, once—horribly—with an enema. "Have you moved your bowels, Arthur?" had been her greeting to him when he came downstairs for breakfast. It had killed his appetite. She'd kept him in short pants, entered his room without knocking, opened—if he should be so fortunate as

6

to receive a letter—his mail. Damn the woman, he thought. Sitting alone in his own outhouse, years and three thousand miles away from her, he felt the back of his neck grow hot.

In the cabin once more, Arthur was unaccountably restless. Usually he accomplished much in the evening and relished his solitude, but tonight even his new book on soils seemed dull and it was too early to sleep. He could mend harness and sharpen tools. Or he could go to the store tonight for his supplies. Saturday was the usual time for storing and gossip. But if he made the trip tonight, he could mail his letter to Emma.

That thought decided him and he prepared a list, took money from the table drawer, and saddled Gray, his horse. They ambled slowly down the trail, and the motion of the beast, and the lively animal and leather smells, soothed him. He stoked Gray's neck and resolved to buy her a lump of sugar. Gray was his first horse, and he liked riding and owning her. He couldn't snake logs out of the woods and drag them to the mill without her help. She was his companion and partner. It occurred to him, riding peacefully along, that she looked a lot like Emma.

Millie Snow, in her black and white checked dress, was tending the counter when Arthur reached the store. A kettle simmered at the back of the stove. The Snows' dog, Jip, a skinny brown mutt, had himself pasted to the floor, flat as a doormat, sleeping in front of it. Arthur was the only customer.

"Doing your storing early, Arthur?" asked Millie in her pert, inquisitive way that reminded him of a chickadee.

"Thought I might as well." He didn't mention the letter. He'd slip it in the slot when the missus wasn't looking. He read her his list of necessities, and together they started to assemble them.

"Harry's off tonight?" Arthur asked.

"Out back. I'll take care of the rest of this. Take a look."

"It's not the new calf already?"

She shook her head no, smugly. "He's a proud man tonight. Go and see."

Arthur stepped through the door into the house and walked through the Snows' kitchen to the back. There was Harry, with three lanterns lit in the yard. In front of the shed shone a buggy: new, black, glittering like a gun barrel, the only buggy North Falls had ever seen.

7

"Well, Harry," Arthur said, impressed. "Well!"

Harry nodded and smiled and the two men stood in silent admiration, hands in their pockets, before the wonder of the vehicle. Once Harry reached out to touch it. Then his hand sank back into his pocket to massage his thigh.

"Guess how much that set me back," Harry finally said to Arthur, but Arthur was lost in a memory. He was thirteen again, a sprouting though reedy boy, and he was going into town with his mother. He wore his suit—knickers, jacket, and cap all of the same herringbone material. They were to pay a call on his grandparents, and Arthur, who had just figured out where babies came from and—more important—how they got there, was feeling very much a man.

"Let me drive the buggy," he said to his mother as she came down the steps fastening her cloak.

She stopped and stared at him aghast, as though he had exposed himself there on the front porch right next to the street. He glanced down to make sure his fly was buttoned.

"Certainly not," she said. "The very idea." With down beginning to show upon his cheeks and chin, Arthur was forced to sit wheezing beside his mother while she whipped up Brownie, the horse.

"Horse dander," she'd said to him for the thousandth time. "It's horse dander that brings on your asthma."

"Guess how much I paid," Harry demanded again.

"I haven't a notion," Arthur said.

"A bundle," Harry said, hugely satisfied. "It cost me a bundle, forty dollars, but ain't she a dandy? Ain't she a beauty? Worth every penny, it is. Worth a fortune."

"Your order's ready, Arthur," chirped Millie Snow in the doorway. He tore himself away, followed her back through the house, and paid up.

"He's gone daft over that thing," Mrs. Snow confided. "Would you keep an eye on the counter? I'm going out there and try to get him to put it up. All those lamps burning, just to gape at a buggy." She shook her head at the waste of kerosene and fluttered off.

Arthur stood in the empty store. The kettle hummed. Jip opened an eye, flapped his tail once, and then subsided. Arthur took the letter out of his pocket, and as he did, a picture came to him. He and Emma were in that buggy, being drawn by Gray. It was a clear spring day. Emma wore a fine hat and a ruffled dress. Her arm was linked through Arthur's arm. She smiled, and her teeth, though prominent and large, were white and wonderful. Gray stepped proudly; Arthur held the reins lightly in one hand. It was Saturday afternoon, and everyone was in town, and Arthur and Emma drove, from one end of the rutted street to the other, past the horse pond, slowly past the store and the Odd Fellows' Hall. They skirted the muck hole and trotted on past the pile of decaying timbers, stacked there for a blacksmith shop that never came to be. In the best of their finery, they drove up to the Methodist church, where Arthur pulled up, jumped down, and helped Emma out.

He walked to the kettle now and held the letter in the steam. The glue released the flap. Delicately he pulled out the letter. Millie Snow had a pen on the desk behind the counter.

P.S. he wrote underneath his signature. His hand was trembling slightly, but he took a deep breath and brought it under control so his penmanship would not betray him. *Why don't you give this place a try? These trees I'm felling bring a decent price. I'll send you the money for a train ticket. I'm absolutely serious. If you like what you see, we'll get married.*

He heard Millie Snow arguing with Harry in the kitchen, as he quickly resealed the letter and dropped it in the slot marked "Mail."

9

II

EMMA HOWE woke before dawn to the tune of Aunt Clothilde snoring through the wall. A slate gray sky outlined the black branches of the elm outside her window and the stars were fading. The sun would be up in half an hour.

Though she often woke early, today she took it as a lucky sign. For the past twenty-four hours, she had been trying to write to Arthur, but her spirit had been agitated and her body heavy. Yesterday she'd had a tender spot in the left side of her abdomen, sensitive to the touch, and all day was peckish and unwell. Today she felt much better.

The unfinished letter lay on the table by the window, next to her most valued possession, her sewing machine. Spring and fall, she worked for people in the area, making up shirts, dresses, and linens. Her father permitted it—even encouraged her—though she was still under his roof and care. Once for the better part of three years she'd run her own dressmaking shop until family duties made her close it. She didn't much like to sew. It was fussy work. But she liked having her own money.

She lighted the candle by her bed, shivered, and put on her wool wrapper and slippers. She was determined to try the letter one more time. In the silence of the morning, the cane-bottomed chair creaked when she sat down, though she had never topped a hundred pounds. Sorry, chair, she thought, and with that flash of whimsical apology realized that she did, indeed, feel like herself again.

Yesterday she'd gotten as far as: *Warwick, Vermont, January 11, 1905 My dear friend Arthur.* Now she crossed out *11* and

10

wrote *12.* She thought for a minute, trying out a sentence or two in her mind. She bit her lip, stared out the window. She chewed the end of the pen, then laid it down. Her brain had turned to mush. She couldn't think what to say.

Her exhaled sigh made a visible cloud in the chilly air. Outside, the world was covered—had been covered, would be covered for weeks—with three feet of snow. She gathered up her clothes and letter. She closed her bedroom door softly and paused, candle in hand, as she passed Aunt Josephine's room, but there was, thank goodness, no sound of familiar, interminable muttering. She slipped down the twisting back stairs, feeling pleasantly like a burglar. The kitchen, after the unheated second floor, was cozy. She made up the fire and hung her clothes to warm. She lighted a lamp, blew out the candle, filled and put on the kettle. Soon Roland Banks, the hired man and her old school fellow, would be bringing in the milk and wanting his breakfast. But she had half an hour free. She pulled the chair with the writing arm close to the heat and faced the all but empty page. She knew what she was supposed to tell Arthur, and she had pretty much accepted it, but she didn't want to say it. It seemed mean, unfriendly, and much too final. She didn't want her present situation—that of a woman who had been proposed to!—to end.

It had been a week since Arthur's invitation came, six days since the Sunday dinner where the clan had agreed on its impossibility. Emma had told her mother about it first, after church while they were dishing up the dinner. Ma—Frances Walker Howe—had a habitually tired face and blue eyes so pale they looked bleached. Emma had thought of her mother as a kindly person in the past, but in recent years Ma had not had much energy for kindness or really for anything else except a dogged following of familiar paths. It seemed, upon hearing Emma's news, that Ma looked even more washed-out and weary.

"I only want what's best for you, Emma," she'd said. "But I don't think this is wise. No woman should marry so far from home. And a total stranger."

"He's not a total stranger," Emma had replied. "You know we've been writing to each other since last June."

11

Ma had looked as blank as unmarked snow, though Emma knew she'd seen the Washington postmarks arriving in the mail. "But you've never laid eyes on him."

"He sent me his picture." With reluctant pride, Emma handed it over.

In sepia tones, Arthur looked steadily into the camera. He wore a collarless shirt, loose pants tucked into his boot tops, suspenders. His hair, receding at the temples, was clipped short as a chain gang prisoner's. He had a high forehead, long nose, small ears, noticing eyes, an open, almost cocky stance. One hand held the bridle of the horse beside him, the other, a narrow-brimmed, high-crowned felt hat. He stood next to a knee-high stump as big as a dining table. In the background the land was stubbled with other smaller stumps. To one side stood a very small house, part log, part frame. At the bottom of the photograph, Arthur had written in his careful hand, "Me and Gray."

The left corner of Ma's mouth gave a downward twitch. "He looks like a farm laborer," she had said. "Like Roland Banks. He could at least have dressed himself up to have his photograph taken. You say he's a homesteader?"

"He's cleared his ranch and built his house himself. He sells vegetables, fruit, butter, and milk to the logging camps."

"He's from Boston?"

"Somerville," said Emma. "His father had a hardware store."

"And now all at once he wants to get married, based on writing you a letter or two? . . ." Ma had covered her mouth with one hand as though her flesh could conceal her thoughts, and her voice had trailed off. "I wonder what he sees in you. . . ."

"For heaven's sake, Ma," said Emma, stung. "He evidently sees a good deal, enough to ask me to come."

"Did I say something wrong?" Ma murmured. "I was just talking to myself. Anyway, Emma, you'll have to ask your pa. Though I say again, it doesn't seem wise. So far from home and a stranger. Your pa and I went to school together, and our families knew each other for three generations. My best friend married your pa's cousin and Pa's grandmother and my grandfather started our local chapter of the Grange. Then there was—"

"I'll ask Pa," Emma had said.

"Wait till he's had his dinner."

Emma had planned to speak to Pa privately after the meal when the rest of the family had scattered into the many rooms of the house for their various naps and escapes from each other. Pa served the chicken stew. Ma served the vegetables. As soon as everyone had food and Pa had said grace, Ma swept the assembled Howes with an excited glance. Emma thought Ma hadn't looked this lively since the younger sister of one of Emma's classmates, Freddie Frye's little sister, fell through the ice at the mill pond and drowned.

"Emma's had a proposal of marriage," Ma had announced. "From a homesteader in the state of Washington. What do you think of that!"

Emma could have killed Ma for blurting it out.

Right away, Pa caught Emma's eye. "What's this?" he asked. There was no way but to explain it all to him in front of everybody.

Immediately Aunt Josephine held forth, her white bun of hair bobbing, though not a single hair dared to emerge from the net that held them trapped inside. Her pince-nez glittered on the narrow bridge of her nose where it pinched so tightly it left red marks. Emma had always thought those marks must hurt, but if so, Aunt Josephine never gave the least sign, not so much as an occasional rub. "Suppose this Mr. Smollett proves to be, as he undoubtedly will, unsuitable? Suppose he changes his mind?"

"He won't—" Emma began, but was cut off as Aunt Josephine's well-manicured hand sliced right down to the table-cloth.

"You'll be far from home, alone and friendless in a strange place, a raw, crude, pioneer town. People will think the worst, and they will have reason to. You will be in a most unfortunate and compromising position. On no account should you consider this a serious offer."

Josephine Howe, before her marriage to Captain Tewkesbury, had been a teacher in a Boston school for young ladies of good family. There she had honed her naturally imperious style, sending one Cabot and two Lowells to their rooms for imperti-

13

nence. She was the oldest of the Howe family and still referred to Ezra, Emma's father, as "my baby brother."

Anne, Emma's next younger sister, married and living in the village, had come as usual for the family dinner with her infant twins. She had inherited the narrow Walker face and jaw, set with tiny, corn kernel teeth, and was an inch taller than Emma's five feet, a fact she did not let Emma forget. Her husband, Lyman Carter, who often took sick on Sundays, was at home with a hard cold. Anne laughed at the very idea of a man's bidding for Emma's hand. "Did you send him your photograph?" she asked Emma pointedly.

"I did," replied Emma.

"Did Mr. Smollett comment on it?"

"He thanked me." He had said that she had lovely eyes, but Emma knew better than to hand that tidbit of information over to Anne. As well give a cat a mouse to play with till the mouse died of fun.

Anne shrugged her shoulders toward her mother—she'd always been Ma's favorite. "At least," Anne had said, "he knows what he'll be getting."

Maggie, the youngest Howe daughter, married just two months, simpered, jiggling her head to make her sausage curls spring lightly up and down. Then she held her head still and poked a finger in and out of the hollow of one curl.

"Oh, Emma," she said, looking not at Emma, but at her tightly collared, pink-faced husband, Clarence Dean. "Suppose he's not a man to be trusted. Suppose he turns out to be a— Bluebeard!"

The only word of approval came from Aunt Clothilde, Josephine and Ezra's younger sister. She was adorned with the heart-shaped earrings and pin, gifts from her late husband, that she always wore at Sunday dinner. As usual, the pin was not quite clasped and slightly crooked, hanging on her flat blue bosom like a drunk clutching at a wall. She squeezed Emma's hand and whispered, "So romantic," but since Clothilde had "spells" and was classified by the family as "soft," her support was worse than useless. The aunts were both Civil War widows, but because her husband had attained the rank of major, Aunt Clothilde's pension was slightly larger. It was her only edge

14

over Josephine and she made the most of it, which Josephine could not bear. The day the pension checks arrived in the mail was a day of tantrums and spells. Pa hid out in the barn or fields. Ma stayed in her room. Emma administered Lydia Pinkham's to Clothilde, "pleasant to the taste, immediate in its effect, a sure cure for Falling of the Womb." To Josephine, she provided witch hazel compresses and medicinal brandy.

Ezra Howe applied himself to the chicken, a tough old biddy that stewing had beaten down but not defeated.

"We'll talk about it after dinner," he said, and Emma breathed a sigh of relief. The nasty cracks made by her sisters and the remarks of her aunts didn't matter. It was Pa who loved and understood her. It was his opinion, and only his, that counted.

After everyone had eaten a raised doughnut floating in maple syrup for dessert, because with church nobody had had time to make cake or pie, Pa took Emma into the parlor, where Anne's two babies, swaddled like butcher's bundles, slept in the old fringed pram. He closed the door and again Emma felt comforted. This was her own pa, who never said no to her, who always took her part. She loved to look at him. He was fifty-nine, of medium height, and slender ("much too thin," his sisters clucked). His close-cropped hair was white. His full, drooping moustache was mostly brown. His eyes, under bushy gray brows, were large and dark, like hers, and his teeth, when he was young, had been as prominent as hers. His sisters said he was "much improved" by the dentures he now wore. Even in January his skin was tanned from working outdoors in all weathers. Today Emma noticed the creases of age as well, but his heavy brown tweed suit was twenty years old and showed no wear, for Pa was easy on clothes, shoes, people. He had flashes of temper, but Emma knew he mostly liked to make her happy.

Today, though, he seemed ill at ease, hidden inside his heavy suit coat, not present to her in his usual way. He did not meet her gaze. He fiddled with his handkerchief and blew his nose, which did not really need blowing.

"You seem to know a good deal about Mr. Smollett and to feel he's a valuable friend."

"I do. I think he's my 'best and truest friend.' " She blushed at

15

quoting her favorite part from one of Arthur's letters. She also blushed because she wanted to say "except for you," but thought it would not sound right.

"I'm glad you have such a friend," Pa said, "but after all, you know him only through his letters. You're such a help to us, Emma. We all depend on you. Your mother's poorly and can't spare you, as you know. Mr. Smollett seems a decent, energetic man, but I'm afraid I can't give my consent, not to a courtship based on letters."

"But Pa—" Emma began. She wanted to tell him, somehow, that she could not—should not—spend her life taking care of elderly aunts instead of her own children.

"I could not rest easy in my mind if I were a party to your going," he said, holding up his hand to fend off her protests. "I could not bring myself to drive you to the station. If Mr. Smollett is in earnest, let him come here and ask for your hand like a gentleman. You've always been my best girl, Emma. Anne is no cook and Maggie can't sew and neither one is as bright as you. You have your little business as a seamstress. You have a way with the aunts. No one can settle them down as you can. You'll always have a home here where you are safe and comfortable and cared for."

It was on the tip of her tongue to ask—and what about when you're dead and gone?—but then he had finally engaged her eyes and had given her his special look, the one he gave no one else in the family, a secret look of conspiracy. It said: we two understand each other. Today she thought it also said: don't leave me, in an almost pleading tone. It had made her not want to argue with him.

"All right, Pa," she said. She had had nothing more to say.

Comfortable in the kitchen now, she *did* feel safe and cared for. She dressed rapidly in her warmed clothes. She heard a mew at the door connecting the house to the ell to the barn and let in Tom, the white barn cat. She set a bowl of scraps on the floor and watched him sniff, then pick and sample. With his thick neck blending into his thick shoulders, and his dainty approach to the bowl, he looked like a prizefighter eating tea sandwiches. She put a pot of coffee on the stove and beat up a batch of biscuits, measuring lard, flour, and milk from memory.

16

Once the biscuits were baking, she returned to her chair and letter.

Tom leaped to her lap, burrowing under her floury apron, making a warm lump. When she stroked his plushy winter fur underneath the cloth, his rattling purr sent vibrations up her fingers into her arm. Looking at her rounded lap, she imagined, as she sometimes did, that the bulge was an unborn child. She thought of Arthur. After he had signed himself her "best and truest friend," she'd written that she knew no other person as well as she knew him. She thought she could tell from his letters he was a gentle man, if not the "gentleman" her parents wanted. He was a hard worker. He had a life he'd asked her to share. He could give her children.

Yesterday, laboring under the heaviness of her body and the full weight of her family's disapproval, she'd tried to figure out what to say. Today she thought she could write the letter. She'd say she wanted to come but that her father didn't approve. Surely Arthur would see that she would come if she could—but that she couldn't. She wouldn't tell him the rest—that she had almost decided she was grateful to Pa for saying no, so she could hide behind his decision. Because even if Pa had said yes, she would have been afraid to go. A moment in the past prevented her.

As a girl, she had taken a trip in October across Lake Champlain on the sidewheeler steamboat *A. Williams* with her Sunday school class. It had been a thrilling adventure. First, the journey to Burlington. Then the ferry ride across the bright blue lake, with sandwiches and new Jonathan apples brought from home. From the center of the lake, Emma had opened her heart to color: flame-colored maples, ash trees of gold, and earth-brown oaks, all intermingled with the blue-green of the conifers.

After a short tie-up at the dock in Port Kent, New York State (she had never been out of Vermont before!), the class had boarded the ferry again and recrossed the lake. They bought their supper (sausages, potatoes, sauerkraut, and cider) extravagantly on board ship. The sun slipped down behind the broad peaks of the Adirondacks in crimson splendor. Emma thought she'd never seen anything so lovely, until closer to home the harvest moon, big as a dinner plate, had risen over the chiseled profile of Mt. Mansfield: a man's forehead, nose, and lips, ending in the north with the stately chin. Emma thought the mountain looked like Pa. The boat thrust itself home through the dark water while the moon dappled the ferry's wake with silver.

She'd stood enchanted at the railing with her cousin Hannah Walker and Roland Banks, members of the Sunday school class. A drunk had stumbled over, thrust his beery face into hers, and loudly observed in a tone of deepest wonder: "You have the biggest teeth I have ever seen." She had tried to walk away, but he pursued her. Without belligerence, but fixed on his stated theme, he appealed to the other passengers. "Don't she?" he'd said, somewhat slurred. "Have you ever seen the like?" And then again, to Emma, "You have the biggest teeth in the world."

Finally she escaped, her face burning, into the ladies' lounge, but not before she heard the guffaws and whispers. Hannah offered her handkerchief and a piece of licorice. When Emma had collected herself, and the two girls emerged, Roland Banks had held a note out to her in his hand. *"I'm sorry, Emma. It's not true. Your friend, Roland,"* the note said. Roland Banks stuttered. He had written her a note because he couldn't trust himself to speak. By consigning her to the world of freaks and cripples, his note had only made things worse.

Sitting now with her unwritten letter to Arthur, Emma imagined her arrival in the tall woods of Washington and the look on Arthur's face as he turned away. He would turn away from her, with laughter or—worse—disgust. She seized the pen and started to write fast and furiously, choosing a formal, complex style, not at all like her usual letters. Upset by this sudden activity, Tom leaped out of her lap, looking peeved.

Your letter, with its suggestion that I come to Washington with the intention of—if we agreed, after a suitable time to become acquainted—forming our marriage, caused much consternation in my household, as you can, I am sure, imagine. My family has expressed many strongly held opinions, all, I am sorry to say, negative. I will not go into each and every one here —it was difficult enough for me to hear them the first time—but suffice it to say that my mother cannot do without me and my father does not give his consent.

18

Although I am hardly a girl, and not, as you know, entirely subject to their governance (by virtue of my ability to make my own way, at least to some extent, through my skill at sewing), I am sorry to tell you that I must refuse your offer. As for my own feelings on the matter—my doubts and apprehensions—I am sure that you can guess them, and they are, perhaps, best left unspoken here.

A rap at the door from the barn startled her. She looked up to see Roland coming in with the milk.

"Roland," she said. "Good morning."

He nodded. He smiled. He set down the milk. He waited, as he always did, for her to offer coffee and biscuits. Sometimes— rarely—he would talk to her. Maggie used to plague him and Anne mimicked his halting speech, but Emma had always been decent to her old schoolmate.

"Sit down and warm up," she said.

He sat, unbuttoned his coat, placed his large hands on his knees, and smiled at her again. He cleared his throat. He was going to talk today.

"I hear you're getting m-m-married, Em-m-ma," he said. "I'll m-miss you. But I wish you well and happy." The last sentence, free of the dreadful letter *m*, came out intact. His congratulations thrilled her, and she responded warmly.

"Why, Roland. How did you know?"

"Clothilde told m-m-me."

He looked so admiring, as though she were already a bride, that she was stunned. Roland found her attractive, could see her as a married woman! She imagined standing before a minister with Arthur and her cheeks grew pink.

"Take off your coat," she said, wanting to take care of him, and he did.

She poured him coffee, dipped cream from the top of the pail and put it in a pitcher, pushed the pitcher and sugar bowl toward him. She took the biscuits from the oven and served him three, split and steaming on a china plate with a chip out of one green edge. The butter stood in a bowl, near the raspberry jam and honey. Some days Roland had honey on his biscuits. Some days, jam. The ordinary ritual of giving Roland breakfast suddenly seemed not ordinary in the least. She wondered how she

19

could leave behind the fat, two-eared sugar bowl and the exact blue-green of the plate edge.

"You don't think it's a bad thing, Roland? To leave home and go all that way to marry a stranger?"

"He can't be a stranger. Not with all those l-letters I've carried up from the village. He m-m-must think a lot of you to write so often."

"You don't think I'm a fool? My father doesn't like it. He says he won't drive me to the station."

Gravely, Roland took a sip of coffee. He had the air of a man who had been, for a lifetime, saving up something important to say. "I'll drive you to the station," he said, plain and clear.

It's not true, Roland's note had said, all those years before. Surely she could convince Pa. He had always encouraged her. They had scarcely ever fought, only once, about Paul Goddard, a subject they had never mentioned again. She had assumed that for Pa the matter of Paul was over and forgotten. It didn't make sense for Pa to disappoint her now.

She smiled broadly, something she rarely allowed herself to do, so shy was she of revealing the teeth she felt ashamed of.

"Roland," she said. "Thank you. I'll talk to Pa tonight. Perhaps he just needed time to get used to the idea. I hope I'll have a letter for you to take down with the milk tomorrow. Let me finish it right now."

She read through what she'd written. In the last paragraph, neatly and so thoroughly that they could not possibly be made out, she crossed out "Although," "sorry," "must," and "refuse." She added the words "But," "so," "happy," and "accept." The rewritten letter now said:

But I am hardly a girl and not, as you know, entirely subject to their governance (by virtue of my ability to make my own way, at least to some extent, through my skill at sewing). So I am happy to tell you that I accept your offer. As for my own feelings on the matter—my doubts and apprehensions—I am sure that you can guess them, and they are, perhaps, best left unspoken here. Let me only say that I have some funds of my own and a friend who will see me to the station. I will come, I will

20

*undertake this journey, and we will see, then, what the future
holds for us both.*
  Your friend,
  Emma

III

T HE NIGHT was bitter, but the kitchen was still warm from the cooking of supper. Emma had washed, dried, and put away the dishes. Ma, sighing like a bellows, had washed and rinsed the dish towels, now steaming on the wooden rack behind the stove. The room smelled faintly of parsnips and Fels Naptha.

Pa was attending a Creamery meeting and the aunts, after five cutthroat games of cribbage, had climbed the stairs to bed, Josephine in triumph and Clothilde in defeat. Tom purred on Emma's lap while she knitted a muffler for Arthur, inspired by the excitement of the afternoon, when all she had been able to think of was him. She was like a cup rounded up over the brim with "being in love." Her revised letter was waiting to be mailed, and now she had to reopen the subject with Ma and Pa, but something had changed for her since she had stamped and sealed the envelope in the presence of her admiring accomplice, Roland. She no longer wanted their permission, but she did very much want their blessing.

"I've been thinking about Mr. Smollett," she said to Ma. "Reconsidering his offer. I believe . . . I believe I may accept after all."

Ma looked up from her eternal mending. She patched and darned. She unraveled wool from old sweaters and knit it into new ones. She made rag rugs and braided rugs, crocheted old stockings into mats for chairs. She made crazy quilts out of scraps and was a little shocked by Emma's using new cloth to make quilts of her own design. As far as Emma knew, the

22

Walkers had never been poor, but they had never been rich, either, and Ma had somehow transformed sensible thrift into a horror of waste that was a way of life. Seeing Ma, one hand holding the sock swelled by the darning egg, her other hand poised with the needle and thread above, Emma felt a pang of pity for the waste of her mother.

Ma seemed neither angry nor surprised at Emma's announcement, but then Emma never could predict her mother's moods. Sometimes a tiny mishap—a spill of cranberry sauce on the tablecloth, a drop of vinegar on a hangnail—set her off and made her natter. Tonight she only licked her thumb and rolled the ends of the thread between her thumb and forefinger to form a knot. As a child, until she learned how easy it was, Emma had thought that a marvelous trick.

"Such a distance," Ma said. "If you travel all that way, you'll be obliged to marry him, like him or not."

It was a better response than Emma could have hoped for. She'd been afraid her mother would say, irritated, "Oh, Emma, I thought that was all settled," or worse, that she'd plead her frailty and need for Emma's help.

"From his letters, I think I'll like him."

"A fancy letter don't make a good husband."

"I suppose," said Emma, sure that her case was the exception.

"Do you know, Emma," said Ma, "that I've never had a room of my own? I shared with my sisters at home, always two to a bed. Then I married your father and shared with him. I shared with my babies when they were born. I've sometimes envied you—your own shop, your own room, your own bed. You've had chances I never had."

Ma's words surprised Emma. The house was large. Three garret rooms, plastered and finished off, were unoccupied except for stored furniture. Why couldn't Ma have used one of them? Emma had always taken having her own room for granted. When she'd been running her dressmaking shop, she had been so caught up in it that she'd been oblivious of her mother's envy or delight. What Emma recalled was Ma's complaining that Emma was no longer around to clean house and do laundry.

"When your friendship with Paul broke off, I can't say I was

23

sorry," Ma said, veering suddenly to a new topic as she often did, following a logic Emma had tried for years to understand and then given up on. The mention of Paul was so startling that Emma, casting on stitches, lost count. Her "friendship" with Paul Goddard was a taboo subject. He had come down from Quebec one summer and Pa had hired him to help with the hay. Emma, nineteen, had fallen hard for him. Paul had lived with his aunt and uncle, who had long ago yielded to Yankee custom and become the Góddards, but Paul had insisted on the French pronunciation of his name with the accent at the end. French Catholics were not popular in Warwick, where they were seen as a threat, especially when they made no attempt to blend in. Paul's being a French Catholic was the reason the romance foundered.

"I thought you wanted all of us to marry," Emma said. She had been happy to make Maggie's wedding cake and dress, but it had not been pleasant to be the oldest unmarried daughter at her youngest sister's marriage.

"Not a Canuck farmhand. Or a Washington homesteader."

"Who, then? It's not as though I had a dozen chances."

"Sometimes nothing's better than something."

"I don't think Arthur Smollett is nothing," said Emma, annoyed.

"The burden you carry can be easier than the burden you don't." Emma visualized Ma's utterance cross-stitched on a dismal sampler, dull black floss on gloomy brown linen. Her mother's resigned caution made her want to scream. Her casting on picked up force and speed and she spoke crisply, with more conviction than she really felt.

"Nevertheless, I've decided," she said, as though they'd been discussing which kind of pickles to make the next day. She finished casting on and laid down her knitting needles with a little triumphant flourish. "I plan to go to Washington as soon as I can get ready. I'll wait up for Pa and talk to him when he gets home tonight. I've written to Arthur to say I'm coming. I have money, and Roland will take me to the train."

"I don't know why you bother to consult me, then," said Ma, "since it's all decided. My opinion don't count."

Emma remembered the time when Ma had stood helpless

24

before the raging aunts. Emma, age fifteen, had stepped between them and stopped the scratching and hair pulling. *My mother doesn't know what to do,* she had thought then, and with that recognition of Ma's incompetence had come an accompanying loss: if Ma couldn't cope, Ma could neither love her nor wound her. Ma's complaints and criticisms, after that afternoon, had become like insect bites, briefly painful but gone in the morning. Emma knew Ma would never say that she'd miss her or promise to come and visit if Emma were ever sick or in trouble. She was just too worn out. Still, she yearned to have her mother approve. "I haven't mailed the letter yet, Ma," Emma said quietly. It was as close as she could come to saying: please, wish me well. She reached out to take Ma's hand, but Ma waved her away.

"You'll go ahead and do as you please, just as you always have. Your father's spoiled you."

This familiar accusation aroused in Emma both injury and pride. To be "spoiled"—soft as bad meat, useless as rotten vegetables—was the worst condemnation where thrift and self-denial earned the highest esteem. But if Pa had spoiled her, it was, Emma thought, because he loved her best, better than Anne, or Maggie, or even Ma. So though her mother's words stung, they also brought on a secret gloat. She waited for Ma's predictable next remark.

"You should have been a boy," she said, compressing her lips into a downward curve and frowning deeply at the darning egg. "If you'd been a boy, your looks wouldn't have mattered. You wouldn't have gone off and left me, and your father wouldn't have made you his pet."

"But I'm not a boy."

"No, you're not," said Ma, glancing at Emma in mock and mild surprise, another of her baffling shifts of mood. She feigned a little yawn. "I believe I'll go up to bed. Since you're waiting up for your father." She even gave Emma a small apologetic smile, as though her earlier cutting speeches had just been recited by rote, as though she was, in a peculiar way, happy to concede victory to Emma. *You want to cater to your Pa?* her smile seemed to say. *Thank you, dearie—then I don't have to.*

Ma tossed her final remark over her shoulder as she left the kitchen by the back stairs, candle in hand. "Of course you don't have to marry Mr. Smollett," she said. "You can always come back."

"Good night, Ma," Emma said, hurt but mostly exasperated. She didn't want to hear one more of Ma's contradictory responses to her decision to leave. But she felt now, more urgently than when she had impulsively rewritten her letter to Arthur saying she would come, that she had made the right choice. No matter what happened in North Falls, no matter whether Arthur was a devil or a saint, it was time to leave home.

Pa worried her, though. She hoped he would relent and give her his blessing. She wanted to lay her head on his chest, feel his hand on her hair, hear his voice saying, "There, Emma. It will be all right. Of course you should go. You and Mr. Smollett will be happy."

She shooed Tom through the woodshed into the barn for the night and then put the kettle on against her father's arrival, adding a new stick to the fire. The clock ticked, the bark on the stick crackled, her knitting needles clicked. These peaceful sounds failed to soothe her. Should she ask him? Tell him? He'd already said, mildly enough, that he would not give his consent. She was afraid of his rare but explosive temper. She knitted and waited, trying to devise a plan.

She remembered approaching Pa about the shop, a storefront in the village she'd gotten through Ma's brother, Albert Walker, her cousin Hannah's father. It was the fall after Paul Goddard had gone away, leaving Emma numb with grief. Uncle Albert, visiting one October night, had remarked that he had lost his tenant, and the idea of the shop had struck Emma like a crash of thunder waking her in the night. She wanted to do it. She had to do it! She'd rushed out, coatless into the windy yard, to ask excitedly if he would lease the space to her. Uncle Albert had laughed and said she was a pushy woman but that yes, he would, and since she was family "and so plain" he'd give a discount on the rent.

Recalling his words, she winced, even now, remembering how she'd bitten back a smart reply because she'd wanted what he had to give. But the lesson had hurt her throat, hard and rough as a plum pit swallowed by mistake: a man could be as homely as you please, and unclean in his habits and uncivil in his speech, but still he could pass remarks about a tidy, bright but buck-toothed woman. Uncle Albert's whiskers were as patchy as a badly mown field and the skin showing through them was red and scaly, but he was a man and the landlord of "the block" on Warwick's main street, and she'd had to let him sneer.

She had asked Pa's permission and he'd readily given it. He had helped her to outfit the shop with shelves and a cutting table. He even offered a cash advance to help her buy her first bolts of sheeting, lining, and interfacing. He advised her about how much to charge and how to keep accounts.

Not long ago, advising Anne about the future upbringing of her new twin babies, Ma had announced to the whole family that "Pa had only spanked Emma once"—as though that accounted for Emma's bad behavior ever since. Emma remembered the spanking as the most terrible thing that had ever happened to her in childhood. She'd run away crying—from betrayal, not just childish tears. She had hidden in the barn so well that neither Ma nor Pa could find her, though they hunted and called. Finally Clothilde had lured her out, like a little injured animal, with a bowl of bread and milk. "Your Pa couldn't bear it," Ma had said, as though she had seen a grave flaw in his character that day and had never forgiven or forgotten it. "He said he'd never whip Emma again and he never did." He had become her special champion. When Emma went to the first day of first grade, he had walked her to the school, holding her hand in his large callused one, making her feel safe, strong, and even pretty, because of the huge white bow perched on her head like an enormous moth that he had admired as they walked along.

Pa had taught her how to milk and weed, how to sharpen an axe and use a drill and hatchet. When she was ten, he let her slide down the big hill with the boys, over Ma's protests, and in high school, he encouraged her to do well in all her subjects and to beat Freddie Frye and win the mathematics prize. Was that what Ma meant by "spoiling" her? Emma had thought it was loving her. The only time he had refused her was in the matter of the barn dance and Paul Goddard.

Emma drew in a sharp breath at that memory and heard, at

the same moment, Pa's footsteps in the woodshed, saw the shed door swing open as he entered the kitchen. He had been the only male in the household for as long as she had been alive, the only boy between two sisters, the father of three daughters but no sons. To Emma, he was intensely masculine, in his high-cut leather boots, overalls, and collarless flannel shirt. At the end of this day, which had started at five A.M., the male mystery of stubble showed upon his throat.

"Hello, Daughter," he said warmly. His greeting made her glad she'd waited up for him, as she had done often in the past.

"Would you like tea, Pa?" she asked, indicating the steaming kettle.

"Had some after the meeting." He hung up his heavy coat and bent stiffly to remove his boots. "I'll take a mulled wine with you, though, I'm that cold." It was one of their private rituals, which Ma, a strict member of the Women's Christian Temperance Union, did not know of (Emma thought) and would never have approved.

Emma heated the homemade dandelion wine with sugar and half a nutmeg, while he put on an old pair of "house" shoes and seated himself by the fire to warm his hands and feet. Heavy woolen long johns, showing white above his socks, couldn't keep him warm on bitter nights like this—or make him seem less thin. His arms, legs, and torso were as linear as stretched taffy.

He told her about the Creamery meeting while she fetched glasses from the pantry, put silver spoons in them to draw the heat and keep the glass from cracking, stirred the heating wine. The Creamery was a scheme the Yankee farmers were using to control the quality and price of milk. But the French farmers, whom they hoped to shut out, had turned to the Boston market and were doing better than Pa and his friends. Listening to him talk about the Creamery and its troubles was a familiar end to Emma's day, and she enjoyed waiting on him and being his confidant even though the Creamery and its endless internal politics bored her. When she poured the almost boiling wine into the glasses and turned to offer him one, she caught a glimpse of the kitchen scene reflected for a moment in the dim black mirror of the window, which erased the yellow from the wine and the wrinkles from Pa's face. Oh! she thought—we look like an old married couple!

"So we'll keep the price firm till the weather breaks," Pa was saying. "And then we'll see. We all agree, for once, that we can get more for butter then." He tasted his wine, sucking it up noisily with a breath of air to cool it, then drying his moustache with the back of his hand. "That tastes all right. Thank you, Daughter."

All right was one of Pa's highest forms of praise. With one hand slightly shielding her teeth, Emma smiled. "Pa," she said, "I've been thinking more about Mr. Smollett in Washington and his invitation that I should come. Do you really think it's a bad idea? For me to go, I mean?"

She was surprised to see how fast his face darkened. "I do," he said firmly. He drank more deeply, then set down his glass. "There's to be an assessment," he said, "We need a new separator, Ralph tells us. I told him if he'd taken proper care of the one we've got, it would still be running and we'd all be a bit richer. Damn fool don't know how to look after machinery and never did."

It was unusual for Pa to swear. Emma knew she was forcing the issue, but she had to find out. He couldn't just go on talking about his assessment and separator when her future hung in the balance. "Why is it bad for me to go?" she asked.

He looked up at her, surprised. In these late night kitchen talks, she realized, he talked and she listened. She sympathized, soothed, and assented. She did not challenge his authority. It occurred to her that long ago she had written off Ralph at the Creamery as a fool on Pa's say-so, though she had never had more than six words with the man or witnessed his behavior for herself. The closeness she had felt for Pa on these late night talks—perhaps she and he weren't as close as she had always imagined.

"Never mind why," he said. "The reasons are clear to anyone with sense." He finished his wine and held out his empty glass as a signal that he wanted more. It was unusual for him to have a second glass. He often told her that one glass was enough to fuddle his wits. Silently she filled his glass a second time.

29

"You think the trip is dangerous, that it's too far, that Washington is too full of Indians and too wild?"

"I think it is not proper."

"Pooh, proper," she said playfully. "I'm not afraid of what people think and never have been. Leave proper to old-fashioned women like Maggie and Anne."

Ordinarily he liked a show of spirit from her, but tonight she saw the color mount in her father's cheeks. He set his glass down with a thump and looked at her angrily. The eyes she so loved and trusted were dark and hard, as strange and threatening as the black ice that formed over the treacherous shallows at the edge of the pond.

"Those French farmers are going to drive us out of business," he said. "Those ten-gallon cans are going down on the train every day. Our Jerseys with their small udders can't compete in quantity. They make a fine, rich creamy milk, not like that blue watery stuff a Holstein gives—but what do city folk know? On the Boston market, that stuff passes for milk and brings a good price. The Creamery can't hold on much longer. You know that, don't you?"

"What does that have to do with—?"

"It is not *proper,*" he said, "to go to a barn dance with a Catholic Canuck. It is not *proper* to sneak out behind your father's back and meet the Canuck at a dance, to dance with him for everyone to see, to carry on, drink French cider, for all I know bed down with him behind a haystack. And it is not *proper* to run after Mr. Smollett like a bitch in heat, to the other side of the country, only to have him make use of you and then abandon you. I take care of my own. I won't have it. Let him come here if he wants you."

"But Pa—"

Pa's face was as flushed as it was the day after the barn dance. Emma had never seen him so angry and out of control as he had been then, and that time he had had no wine to drink. It had been a Sunday, with all the family present, and Pa's words had rung in her ears: "I'll have him horsewhipped," he raged, "and you, Emma—how could you throw yourself away, give yourself to that mongrel dog?"

"Don't 'But Pa' me," Pa said now. "Stand up! Stand up, I say!"

30

Dumbfounded and afraid, Emma stood, and he stood with her.

"Look at you," he said more quietly. "You're beautiful to me because I love you, but you're a plain girl, Emma. No man will ever want you—only till he's satisfied, which don't take long. But you're my daughter. You're mine. I'll take care of you, and I'll never lay a hand on you, I swear."

He held out his arms, as he had done when she was a child, and she longed to run into them and sob away her pain and confusion, holding him tightly around the waist. But she remembered the week after the dance, how he wouldn't speak to her until the next Sunday came. Then after church he had held out his arms to her, in reconciliation. Needing his forgiveness, she'd gone to him, but the embrace was all wrong. She couldn't put her arms around his waist like a little girl anymore, not after having been with Paul. She had hated the feel of Pa's body, the scent of his breath, the way he had hugged her too hard, hurting her breasts, had held her too long though she had tried to pull away. Afterwards, Maggie had told her, "He winked, Emma. Over the top of your head, he winked at us. As if none of it mattered after all, as if it was all a joke. Why did he wink like that, when he'd been so angry with you and hated Paul so much?"

Now Emma could not move. She stared at Pa as though he were a stranger. He looked pitiful and hateful, holding out his arms that way. Her throat swelled with tears, but she fought to keep them down. If she cried, she would run to him for comfort —she wouldn't be able to stop herself.

"Pa," she said, mastering her voice with difficulty. "I've received a proposal from an honest man. I'm going to accept it. I'll travel to North Falls as soon as I can get myself packed. Paul Goddárd has nothing to do—"

"GODdard!" he said fiercely.

"I'm going, Pa."

"Then go and be damned to you. I'm done." In a sudden motion his right hand swept the empty glass from the table, hurling it against the iron stove. It shattered; the dregs of wine hissed, hitting the hot metal. Emma watched her father stride from the room, banging the door behind him. Her knees were trembling and she sat down shakily in her chair.

As she sat, trembling and fighting tears, she remembered how, only this morning, Roland had sat in the chair Pa had just left empty, and she held onto Roland's admiration as though it were a life preserver in a lake hit by a hurricane. Roland stuttered, but he wasn't stupid. He was the best hand with animals in the area—even Pa said that Roland could settle an upset beast no matter what the cause. She had seen Roland lean on the shoulder of a lame horse to get it to shift its weight from its injured hoof and then pull a nail from the hoof with a pair of pliers, letting the pus run free so the hoof could heal. Roland could do that, even though, as Pa said, a horse didn't have enough brain to be grateful. . . .

"Go and be damned to you."

She put her head down on her arms, wanting to cry, but no tears came, only an aching throat and her head shaking back and forth as though saying—No, no. No, Pa.

She got up, swept up the glass, and hid it at the bottom of the waste can away from Ma's prying eyes. No one must know what passed between us here, she thought. She took her candle and climbed the stairs to bed, clinging to the thought of Roland—all these years he had admired her—and to Arthur's words, "Your best and truest friend." She was going to Washington. She would find out if those words were true.

IV

MMA RODE next to Roland, with the lap robe tucked around them. Next to each fence post, moonlight cast faint blue shadows on the snow. The horse's breath came in plumes under the frozen stars. The sleigh's runners squeaked on the hard-packed snow.

As they got further and further from the farm, they left that stark beauty behind. In the dead of winter before sunrise, the village of Warwick was cheerless. Ordinarily, Emma enjoyed a trip to town. Her habit was to spend an absorbing morning in the drygoods store, testing critically between her fingers the textures of rose colored crêpe de chine and crisp yellow cambric, while her eye uncritically relished their colors.

Today the town's color was gray, in various shades. For several days no new flakes had fallen. The snow in people's yards as Emma and Roland approached the outskirts was pocked and dirty. By noon ice spikes shaped like ridged animal horns would drip along southern eaves in the sun, but except for that small sign, there were no hints that spring would come.

Emma's stomach was jumpy from an extra cup of coffee, gulped standing up to keep her warm on the way to the station. She'd known the coffee would make her jittery, but all week, getting ready to go, she'd wanted to heighten the sense of urgency she had about leaving. She'd rushed about—shopping and packing—because hurrying gave her the grit she needed to go through with her decision.

When she'd asked Ma if she should empty the wardrobe and

drawers in her room, Ma had replied in her vague, double-edged way, "Oh, you needn't do that."

Emma hadn't known if Ma meant, "Your room will always be there for you," or "You'll fail out there and be back soon enough." With Ma it was always both—she gave with one hand and took back with the other. Emma had seized upon the second interpretation, well aware that she was doing it, because she wanted to be mad at Ma. She had needed that anger to fuel her fire and keep her moving toward her goal.

So she had stripped the drawers and wardrobe, throwing out threadbare garments and old magazines, worn shoes and exercise books from school. She had left not so much as a hairpin. Her trunk was a model of practicality, containing her sewing machine and folding sewing table, linens, quilts, clothes, shoes, and books—her modest dowry. But at the last minute, just before she'd banged down the lid and locked it, she had laid on top a photograph of the Warwick house with her entire family posed on the porch. Taken on the recent occasion of Maggie's November wedding, it was a poor picture. It had been cold on the porch and the faces looked uncomfortable, as people shivered and squinted into the sun. The bride smirked while the groom looked scared to death. But at least everyone was in it— she could show all of her relations to Arthur at once.

When her trunk was closed, and her valise and bag were full, she had found herself staring at a pile of things she did not want to take and could not bear to throw away: her favorite doll; a locket Anne had given her on Emma's fifteenth birthday containing a snip of hair from Hunter, the family dog, who had died that year; a diary she had kept assiduously during six months of the same year, a gift from Clothilde and pretty dull reading; a granite chip from the top of Stannard Mountain, brought home from a springtime hike with Pa, the day they had seen hundreds of yellow lady slippers blooming out of the ashes of a forest fire; and a goldfinch feather only two inches long but stippled in colors so vivid they took the breath away.

The most painful of these relics was a formal photograph of Pa, taken at Kellog's Studios in St. Johnsbury. His sisters had urged him to pose in his Civil War uniform, but Pa had said that since the Vermont Cavalry didn't even get fired upon while he was in it, his best suit was good enough. Still, he had a soldierly air. He held his narrow head erect like a short-bladed hatchet and sighted into the distance past an aquiline nose set proudly over a horseman's dark, flowing moustache. When he'd given it to her, for her high school graduation, Emma had thought he looked like a cross between Lincoln and Jesus Christ.

Looking at the picture had plunged her into sorrow, until Aunt Josephine's voice in the hallway had broken through. "Others may do as they like," she was proclaiming like royalty to her younger sister, "but I know what's right." "Yes, dear," Clothilde had replied in her sweet little doormat voice. All morning Clothilde had been worrying about what to use as a centerpiece at the altar guild tea that afternoon, where she was "in charge of the table," and as usual Josephine had taken over. Her sadness suddenly gone, Emma had thrown her mementos into a box and rushed to the attic with it, impelled by the same ferocious energy that had carried her through the week.

As she had prepared to leave, Ma, her sisters, and Aunt Josephine had, each in her own way, acknowledged the fact of her departure, though no one except Clothilde really approved. But they wouldn't be a party to her recklessness by seeing her off, nor did she expect them to. She understood that they felt if a person was fool enough to set off for the North Pole in a hot air balloon, you might not be able to stop her, but there was no point in packing her a lunch. What hurt was Pa. He hadn't spoken to her directly since their fight. Last night, when she, Ma, and Pa had been sitting in the kitchen, he'd suddenly announced he was going to bed early and only included her in his general good night to Ma, as though the morrow were a completely ordinary day. His refusing to say good-bye before her journey had made her heart ache and her courage, so much of it contrived, fail. Desperate, she had sent a look to Ma that said: I don't think I can go through with this. Surprisingly, it was the kindly childhood Ma, whose cool hand had smoothed the hair back from her sweaty forehead, that had returned her gaze: Yes, you can. You go on now.

The town, when they finally arrived, was dark except for a light in the police station. On the main street, her old shop, now leased to a stationer, had its blinds drawn. The churches looked

35

as disapproving as Pa's face. Frozen chunks of dirt smeared the snow banks piled shoulder high around the station. "W-watch your step," Roland said to Emma, as she jumped down amid icy ruts dolloped with horse droppings. She gathered her skirts, her bag and valise, leaving Roland to see to her trunk. She went inside to buy her ticket. To get to North Falls, Snohomish County, in the state of Washington, first she had to get to New York.

"Round trip?" the stationmaster asked, peering curiously from beneath his visor. Black garters crimped his white shirt sleeves.

"One way," she murmured and was frightened by the finality of the words. She received her ticket and the bills and coins he handed her and stuffed them into her purse, too shaken to put them away properly or count her change.

She sat on the hard wooden bench, clutching with both hands her purse full of money for the trip, worried about carrying so much cash, even though she had handled sizable sums before. At its peak, her shop had barely kept up with the demand for children's underclothes. Each Friday night she had swept up the cuttings, zig-zagged by the pinking shears, and the lint and threads, into an untidy bird's nest, bright with an occasional pin. She'd salvaged the pins. She'd hooked the shutters, turned off the gas, locked the doors, and taken the week's receipts to the Warwick Trust in a canvas drawstring bag. Freddie Frye, her old classmate, had been one of the bank officers, and it had given her no small satisfaction to make her deposit—sometimes as much as fifteen dollars—under Freddie's snub nose, which in high school had had a piggish look. He was respectable now, wore starched collars and slicked down his bushy hair, had a wife and children, and passed the collection plate in church on Sunday. But in ninth grade he had tormented her.

On the first day of high school at Warwick Academy, when Emma and her classmates returned from the hazy yellow summer, most everyone, all at once, had changed. Some were still well-proportioned, but most of the girls looked lumpy as one feature or another—noses, buttocks, chests—burgeoned ahead of the rest. Many of the boys, like Freddie, had wrists and ankles far longer than their pants and sleeves, which gave them the clownish look of scarecrows. The unconscious ease of childhood ended as they stared at each other's gawky growth. The teasing done that day set the tone for the rest of the year.

"Look at the beaver," Freddie had yelled at Emma across the schoolyard. "How's your dam coming, Beaver? How do the pine trees taste?"

She had stared at her shoe tops as though memorizing the cracks in the leather and counting the buttons on each one.

"Teeth like a beaver, teeth like a beaver," he had sing-songed, until blood heated her high forehead clear up into her scalp and her eyes filled with tears. When a drop made a round clean spot on her dusty shoe top, Freddie was satisfied.

"Aww," he groaned in mock sympathy. "Aww, Emma's a crybaby." He spat onto the hard-packed dirt of the playground, where even during the disuse of summer no weed or flower dared to raise its head, and went off to harass his next victim, Blanche LeCoin. Blanche's father, Emil LeCoin, raised "French cows," Holsteins, the "big milkers." As a Catholic (a "mackerel snapper") and a Canuck, Blanche was fair game. She stood as near the locked school door as possible, waiting to be allowed indoors to safety, her shoulders hunched to hide her suddenly ballooning breasts.

"Watch, watch!" Freddie had called to his cronies. He snatched Blanche's red hair ribbon and dashed away, making her run awkwardly after him so that her melon breasts flopped. She crossed her arms over them to conceal their jiggling, but it was impossible to hide such a thing. Freddie's pals snorted and cackled behind their oversized paws. At the end of ninth grade, Blanche had left school to become a nun.

In the sixth grade spelling bee, Emma had spelled down Freddie Frye with "commitment," leading the girls' team to victory. When Freddie Frye had accused her of cheating and being a teacher's pet, she'd kicked him hard on the shin and yelled, "Damn you, Freddie Frye!" But she was fourteen now and over the summer Ma had outfitted her with clean cloths to catch her monthly, rusty-red blood. She couldn't go around kicking boys anymore. She had promised God not to curse. She had taken the Temperance Pledge.

"Ignore him," Ma counseled, when Emma told of Freddie's

37

taunt. "He'll tire of the game and leave you alone if he don't get a rise out of you." She had smoothed Emma's hair back off her forehead. "It's time to peel the potatoes for supper," she had said.

So Emma had avoided Freddie Frye and tried to ignore him by reciting silent Bible verses. "The Lord is my shepherd," she would say to herself to block out the sound of "Beaver." Or, "I shall lift up mine eyes to hills from whence cometh my strength," standing in the schoolyard and looking fixedly at the purpled sides and snowy peaks of Stannard Mountain, always called just "the mountain." But there was no help for it. She could not keep from blushing, and if she would blush, Freddie would tease. It took ten years for her to look him spang in the eye with her bank deposit and say, "I guess you can handle this, Fred."

"I guess I can, Emma," he had replied. Not Beaver. Emma. Emma Howe.

The purse was full to bursting. Besides all that money, it contained handkerchiefs, a small metal nail file, and a large metal comb with a narrow rat tail at one end. Also a bag of lemon drops from Neilson's store, a box of Smith Brothers' cough drops, and a tiny clear bottle, with a screw top, of Spirits of Ammonia. Emma had never fainted in her life, but for a trip like this it was best to be prepared. The purse also held a small supply of writing paper with envelopes; red, two-cent George Washington stamps; a pen; and a bottle of ink with the cork pressed in so tight she would probably never get it out again. And of course the packet of Arthur's letters, well-thumbed, reread, arranged in chronological order, and tied with a short piece of white grocer's string. Into one she'd tucked a copy of her poem, "Bloodroot," clipped from *Nature's Friends.*

The bag, leaning against her ankle, contained a toothbrush and Dr. Lyons Perfect Tooth Powder, a new cake of Pears soap in its box, a wash cloth, a towel, more handkerchiefs, witch hazel, stockings, flannel drawers and vests, a woolen petticoat smelling of mothballs, a jar of rose-scented glycerine salve, a wooden-handled bag containing the green yarn she was knitting up for Arthur, her sewing (dresses for Anne's babies), a Bible, *A Summer in Arcady* by James Lane Allen in which a young woman's Virtue was pitted against a young man's Nature and won by a whisker, the February issue of the *Ladies' Home Journal*, a package of Antiseptic Sanitary Towels ordered from the Sears catalogue, a tin box of hermits, a packet of ham sandwiches, and a mason jar of tea.

It was a large, heavy bag. It was a large, heavy purse. Her fingers grew numb with gripping it.

Roland joined her, still silent, on the bench. For fifteen minutes they fidgeted in the waiting room, made hot and airless by the wood stove and the gas lights, in company with a brown-clad commercial traveler with sample case and predawn cigar, and a neatly dressed woman accompanied by two small children. The woman's cloak was good navy wool, Emma noted professionally, well-dyed, with pewter buttons shaped like chrysanthemum flowers. Emma admired its simple elegance. The boy, five or six years old, was big-eyed and serious, in gray leggings, cap, and coat. The little girl wore a white knitted outfit —hat with earflaps and a pompom, leggings, and a popcorn-stitch coat. She put her mittened hands over her face and wouldn't look at Emma, but the boy stared intently.

"Good morning," Emma said to the woman, thinking how fortunate she was in her offspring. Acknowledging Emma's admiration of the children, the woman ventured a tiny smile, her lips curving up but her eyes sad. She kept one hand on the small boy's shoulder. When the little girl's nose began to drip thickly, the woman wiped it with a large white cotton handkerchief, already somewhat damp.

The minutes ticked by. The smoke thickened from the salesman's cigar. The tips of Emma's fingers, strenuously gripping her purse, began to ache, and she released the purse to remove her gloves and flex them for a moment. As the blood returned, her fingertips tingled as though they had brushed a nettle.

At last the stationmaster rang the bell and the little band moved out to the frosty air of the platform. Over the mountains, the eastern sky was brightening. Emma shivered and turned toward Roland to see if he had noticed the dawn. He was watching it. He turned to catch her eye. Say something, Roland, she thought urgently. Say, "Things won't be the same around here when you're gone."

Roland's face responded to her silent plea. As a sign of impending conversation, he removed his earmuffs.

"Have you ever b-been to B-Boston?" he asked.

"No," said Emma, surprised. Boston was hardly on her mind right then, but perhaps the whole notion of travel had put it into Roland's. Of course she knew that to folks from Warwick, Boston was the center of civilized life, an impressive blend of good manners, commerce, and the arts. Brown eggs were Boston eggs and to be trusted, whereas white eggs came from New York and could be, for all anyone knew, filled with ink. Boston had Congregationalists and Unitarians, Emerson, and Louisa May Alcott. There was music in Boston, and medicine, Harvard College, Fanueil Hall, Fanny Farmer, and the Red Sox. The drygoods store in Warwick was, in fact, called "The Boston Store."

Roland put the earmuffs in his pocket. "I thought to go to B-Boston once," he said. "I read in the p-paper that a famous doctor at the hospital there was interested in st-st-stutterers. He'd st-st-study you and treat you free."

"Why didn't you go?"

"I thought on it, but it was too far and too risky. The hospital s-sounded f-fancy and the doctor was pr-probably a quack. No use looking for trouble."

"But the doctor might have helped you."

"I m-m-m-might have wound up with no voice at all." He shifted his weight from one foot to the other and cleared a bit of phlegm from his throat. In deference to her presence, he swallowed it instead of spitting.

Emma clutched her purse to her bosom. In one form or another, she'd heard Roland's kind of reasoning all her life, but because she was about to leave, perhaps forever, his words struck her in a new way. If I had taken that point of view, she thought, I'd be in the kitchen right now. How did I escape? How did I have the courage to come this far?

40

V

JUST THEN they heard the engine of the train chugging into town. Smoke billowed, brakes squealed. Everyone looked down the tracks for a first glimpse, as though their eyes had to verify their ears.

"Here she comes," said the commercial traveler. His tone made Emma wonder why the train was female—perhaps because it was driven by a man.

The conductor, with jaunty uniform, dark eyes, and jutting chin, swung down to help the passengers aboard. The woman with the two small children was first, then Emma, then the salesman who had now gotten rid of his cigar. Emma's knees wobbled involuntarily, but then she was distracted from her fear by stooping to boost the boy up the steps, while the conductor, whose index finger was missing from his right hand, helped the mother with the little girl.

"Thank you, Roland," she said. "Good-bye." She took his hand, which she had never touched before, and in a rush of feeling for him that overcame her knowledge that she would embarrass him, pressed it to her cheek. Then she climbed on the train and moved down the aisle.

Even at this early hour nearly every seat was full. She found a seat on the aisle, on the side away from the platform. The man in the window seat helped her stow her valise and then, with a curt "Good morning," dismissed her in favor of his newspaper. He was nattily togged in flecked flannel, spats, a gold watch and chain, and a moustache with waxed ends that pointed up. Emma was relieved not to have to talk to him.

41

Waiting for the train to pull out and wanting to distract herself from the grief of leaving, she concentrated on Roland. She knew he led a lonely life. Except for the minister's handshake on Sunday morning, no one took his hand. He had no family or kin. He worked twelve hours a day, six days a week, and came to milk twice on Sunday. He boarded in town. He didn't drink, play cards, or go to dances—Ma wouldn't have consented to Pa's having hired him if he had. She realized sadly that whole days must go by for Roland, virtually wordless.

She hoisted herself up to look out the window across the aisle, hoping to spot him, wanting to wave good-bye, to express the love and thanks she owed to what she was leaving behind. But when the train pulled out at last and she waved, Roland stood watching with his hands in his pockets and his earmuffs on, apparently not seeing her and not waving back. She settled back into her seat, disappointed.

In the passageway between the cars, the whistle tooted. Metal clanged and the powerful engine chugged.

"Ça bouge," said a nasal French Canadian voice in the seat behind.

The sheds outside the window started moving slowly to the rear and were replaced by more sheds, warehouses, the vast dark bins of Warwick Consolidated Coal. The pulse of the train beat in her ears and her stomach fluttered.

The throbbing of the engine grew less loud and more regular as it rounded a curve between high hills of evergreen and tall banks of snow. The train picked up speed and whirled along, heading for the Connecticut River Valley. Well! she thought, smiling at the newspaper in the seat beside her, suddenly exhilarated, not worrying about her teeth. I'm here! It was like stepping into the rowboat at the dock at Caspian Lake, the green smell of the water all around, the reeds and duckweed, the dock firm, the rowboat bobbing and fragile as a floating leaf. The lake was broad and dotted with whitecaps in a fresh breeze and the boat was going a long way from shore. But if one foot was in the boat, the other had to follow, and inexorably the voyage had begun.

At the front of the car, she saw the woman with the children getting settled.

42

"Ticket, Missy," the conductor said loudly at her elbow. His unexpected presence startled her—she had just started to get her bearings. She wished he'd said "Miss"—that she didn't, because of being small, look younger than she was.

In her wish to seem completely poised and produce her ticket quickly, she pulled it from her purse, flirting out at the same time bills and change. A dollar floated onto her seatmate's narrow knees and a coin, a fifty cent piece from the heavy sound of it, landed with a clunk in the aisle, then rolled along making a little metallic whine. At the sound of money, everyone looked up.

"Oh, dear," Emma said, flushing scarlet. She heard the coin still ringing on its way. People would think she was rich and careless, or poor and silly. She wasn't even out of Vermont yet and already she was making a fool of herself, throwing money around. For someone like Roland, a dollar was a day's wage.

"Allow me," said her seatmate, plucking the greenback from his perfectly creased lap and handing it to her folded delicately between two fingers like a live butterfly.

Too overcome to speak, she ducked her head and put the bill carefully away inside her purse.

The conductor went off after the fifty cent piece and returned after only a moment.

"That youngster that got on with you found it," he reported, dropping the cold silver into Emma's damp palm. "I gave him a toffee and one for his sister, too."

"I'm so sorry," Emma said, blushing again. She felt like a girl from the sticks, a country bumpkin.

"Your ticket, Missy?"

"Oh, yes." She handed it to him at last.

"I'll bet this is your first trip," he said, his eyes glinting under his ridge of brow like coal catching the light in a bin.

"Yes, it is," Emma admitted. With difficulty she managed not to blurt out that she was going all the way across the country, to the end of the earth.

He examined her ticket. "Change for Chicago in New York." The skin on the nub of his missing finger was pink and tight. He saw her notice it.

"Dues," he said, holding up the hand. "The sign of the trade.

43

Show me a brakeman with all his fingers and I'll show you a brakeman who never did a lick of work. Brakes are all set automatic now, but when I was coming up, brakeman was a man's job." He punched Emma's ticket and returned it to her, watching her store it away in her purse in a small leather case.

"That's right, Missy." He moved on, walking the swaying aisle like a practiced deckhand, never having to catch hold of a seat back for support. As soon as he was out of earshot, Emma's seatmate lifted his nose from his newspaper.

"Surely," he said, addressing his remark not so much to Emma as to the air, "mutilation is not in this day and age considered an appropriate prerequisite for manhood."

He retreated immediately into his paper, sparing Emma the necessity of a reply. She realized that like Aunt Josephine, he didn't want to debate, only to render his verdict. For once she was grateful to Aunt Josephine for giving her a way to size up this stranger.

Emma was glad to settle back and rest after the commotion. All her life she'd been brought up to think that the Howes of Warwick were the be-all and the end-all of the world, the Howes and Walkers and their various nearby kin. Outsiders—people from "away"—were to be feared and mistrusted. As children, she and Anne and Maggie had hidden under the table-cloth at the sound of the doorknocker, shy as field mice. She remembered a friend of Aunt Josephine complaining that her family, despite long residence in Warwick, had never been fully accepted.

"I understand that because my husband and I are from out of state, we'll never be considered Vermonters though we've lived here all our lives," the friend had said in plaintive tones. "But our son and daughter were *born* here. It does seem unfair that our children be slighted in this way."

"If your cat had kittens in the oven," Aunt Josephine had said with some asperity, "you wouldn't call them biscuits."

Now Emma was herself "away," and the newness of every-thing was already challenging her notions. The man across the aisle took a gurgling drink from a silver flask and, catching her observing eye, gave her a wink. Instantly, she turned away. She was shocked, but in an odd way she was also pleased. Nobody winked, no matter how drunk, at ugly girls. Pa may have made his crocks of dandelion wine, but Emma's Methodist upbringing by Ma was censorious of alcohol in any form—though Emma had noticed that Ma, true to her contradictory nature, loved brandied fruit cake, rum balls, and the smell of vanilla. Perhaps the man was not drunk, only merry. Of course, he probably shouldn't drink, at least not so early in the day. According to the Methodist tracts, "The consumption of alcoholic beverages destroys the God-given gift of reason, destroys homes, and leaves innocent women and children destitute." But she was curious— what, really, was it like to take a drink?

The man sitting next to the drinker was asleep and snoring lightly, she noted with one judicious glance, carefully aimed to avoid additional winks. This, too, was somewhat shocking. But she herself would be on the train for better than a week. She would eat, drink, go to the toilet, and sleep among a carful of complete strangers. They would yawn, comb their hair, scrape the crusts out of their eye corners, and break wind together. She raised her eyebrows just thinking about it. Past the newspaper at her side, the evergreens raced backwards at thirty-five miles per hour. The pines and spruces at home had never learned to run. Travel really was quite broadening.

Ticka bang, ticka bang, ticka bang clicked the wheels over the railroad ties, stirring as a Sousa march. After twenty minutes of staring fascinated out the window, however, her excitement faded and the coffee she had drunk, hours ago, began to wear off. Under his newspaper her seatmate was catching forty winks. The man with the flask was napping, too. Emma closed her eyes. She thought of the boy who found her coin, the heft of him, the brown hair that lay like silk embroidery floss across his pale forehead. She imagined his and his mother's life, sure that it was admirable, shiny with polish, sweet with love, a *Ladies' Home Journal* life.

Emma slept. When, in a few minutes she awakened, it was to a gentle touch on her arm. The boy, seeking amusement by wandering the aisle, had come to pay a call.

"Hello," he said. "I'm going to live with my grandmother."

"Oh," said Emma, taken a bit aback. "Where does your grandmother live?"

"In New York. She's old, so we must be quiet."

"Have you been to her house before?"

He shook his head, no. His eyes looked older than he seemed because they were so resigned. Behind the resignation was hurt, anger, bafflement.

"And is your sister going to live there, too?"

"Yes. And I'm to make sure she doesn't bother anyone. But Aunt Emily isn't going to stay. She's only taking us there."

"Wilfred?" called the woman's voice.

"My mother died," the boy said. The words spilled out of his mouth like a lesson learned by rote, whose meaning he did not begin to fully grasp. "She had a baby and she died and the baby died, too. My father says he can't keep us anymore."

"Oh, dear. I *am* sorry," Emma said.

The woman—Aunt Emily—came hurrying down the aisle and took Wilfred by the hand.

"Excuse us, Miss," she said to Emma and walked the boy swiftly back to his seat at the front of the car.

So Wilfred had no magazine life. Only a father rejecting him, like Pa when Emma had told him she had decided to go away. Coal and kerosene smoke had made the air of the carriage close, and a cold sweat broke out on her upper lip despite the heat of the train car. All at once she wanted desperately to get off.

This journey was a terrible mistake. She knew nothing about Arthur Smollett, only what he had chosen to tell her in his oh, so neat, oh, so carefully worded letters, only what she had wishfully imagined. She became aware of an unclean smell emanating from the natty flannels of the man beside her and of the sourness of his breath. She wasn't squeamish. She'd killed many a chicken, seen the slaughtering of pigs. She'd watched, through a knothole in the partition of the cow barn, a heifer being bred and a calf being born, had heard the groans of humping dogs under the back yard clothesline. But now her head spun dizzily and she couldn't draw a deep, clear breath. She pressed a handkerchief scented faintly with lavender to her nose, thinking in panic—what have I done? What on earth have I done?

Suppose Arthur chewed tobacco and the juice caught in the ends of his moustache, staining his teeth brown and dripping

46

slimily across his chin? What if he had a bad stomach and his burps smelled like vomit, what if he continually hawked up globs and spat them into the fireplace and sink (if there *was* a fireplace; if there *was* a sink!)? What if he stank like Silly Ned, Warwick's idiot, old Ned Turner's boy, still a five-year-old at the age of fifty, who picked berries in summer and shoveled snow in winter and slept in the livery stable with the horses and lived on the stale bread and rotten vegetables they threw away at Neilson's store? Silly Ned had grabbed her once when she was ten and kissed her—horrible, horrible!—before she could break away. How, she thought, can I marry a man I've never smelled?

47

VI

THE AFTERNOON was getting on toward four when Arthur and Bert Brown, his nearest neighbor, faced the last big stump.

Bert owned the only team of oxen in Snohomish County. Clearing land of stumps and boulders, at $5 a day, kept the team busy and supported Bert's growing family. He had two nearly grown daughters, Elva and Lucy, by his first wife (the second baby, Lucy, was the one that killed her). With his second wife, Dee, he had five children, the fifth born just a week ago. In terms of children alone, he was seen as a solid citizen in sparsely populated North Falls.

"Just that big stump left," Arthur said. They were both tired and filthy after working in the muck all day.

Bert wiped his bulging forehead on his mostly clean upper sleeve, glanced at the dark sky, and said, "Gonna rain. I don't expect we'll get that one."

Bert, a German, had taken Brown as his American last name because his German name was hard to spell and pronounce. He'd told Arthur he had left it behind, along with the Catholic church and the German army, where he'd served for three years before he emigrated. A clean break with the best-forgotten past, Arthur had thought—he knew about that. Somewhere along the way, Bert had also lost most of his hair and four of his front teeth. Arthur imagined the teeth went in a fight. The baldness, plus the pointed incisors framing the empty spot in his mouth, gave him the feral look of a retired but still dangerous

48

wolf. He spat neatly through the spot now to underscore his point and said again, "I expect we'll have to let that one go."

Arthur felt on his mettle around Bert. For one thing, Bert was twenty years his senior and powerfully built, as massive through the neck and shoulders as one of his red-brown oxen. Just the look of the man was a challenge. Arthur didn't hunt and lived alone. Bert was not only an officer in the Old Fellows but also known as a fine fisherman and hunter. He did well the things men were supposed to do—worked for himself, helped develop the community, raised his family. He seemed not to have, as Arthur did, doubts about his manhood. When Arthur was around Bert, Arthur competed, because he felt inadequate. Besides, he'd had that stump at the top of his list all day. If they didn't get it out of there, it would ruin his garden space.

"I don't think we can duck it. If we don't get it, that spot'll be no good to me. I'll never be able to plow it."

They had pulled the smaller stumps in the newly cleared area, working the team around the big one in an irregular circle. Now it stood, stubbornly alone, like the solid hub of a wheel from which they had knocked out the lightweight spokes. It had to go.

"Well," said Bert, "I suppose we could give it a try. But then I wanta get the team home."

Pleased that Bert had agreed, Arthur jumped into the hole he'd dug around the stump and attached the hooks and chain. Bert whipped up the team, and the oxen strained forward, stamping into the moist earth, their haunches straining while the harness creaked with the pull and the chain clanked as it lifted off the earth and bore the stress. Three times, Bert urged the team on, using the whip each time, but though the stump rocked forward, it didn't give way. Arthur knew from experience that Bert didn't force his animals beyond three pulls without a rest.

"No good," Bert said. His look to Arthur added—accept the facts: sometimes the trees win. The rain he had predicted, and that came nearly every day at this time, started to drizzle down. Arthur was hot enough and dirty enough so it felt good. He'd also seen, on the last pull, that the stump was anchored deep into the ground by a big root accessible to an axe only when the

49

team's weight bore the rest forward. If he could get his axe into that root, while Bert kept the team's pressure up, the stump would be out of there—he was sure of it. Of course, it was risky. If the team gave out before he had cut enough into the root, the whole thing would fall back fast and he'd be hard put to get out of the way. They'd used the same method on a few of the others, but those were smaller. This one was the only one whose weight was really a threat.

"Let me get under there and whack that last root, at least make a dent in it," he said. He was frustrated by the failure. Having figured out a scheme, he wanted to prove to Bert that it would work.

"It's chancy," Bert said.

Arthur shrugged to say—it's on me. "One long pull instead of three, Bert. Just give me a bit more chopping time." He took a whetstone out of his pocket and stroked his axe to sharpen the edge. Bert looked impatient. The rain was changing from drizzle to a steady shower.

"You take much longer with that and the team'll slip on the mud. Don't want to carry you home to my missus in a box."

Arthur deliberately whetted the axe six more times. It was one of his few lessons from his dad—keep your tools sharp and use the right one for the job. Still standing in the hole, he carefully put the stone back in his pocket.

"Gee up!" Bert shouted. As the stump rocked, Arthur leaned under and chopped hard and fast, through dirt, through the skin, into the soft flesh, into the iron heart. Over his head, the stump loomed, held up but not moving forward. He heard the team snort as Bert kept them pulling past their normal time. He had a quick vision of his body crushed ignominiously in this ugly hole, and he flailed wildly for a couple of strokes, missing the sweet center spot. Then he got control again and made his strokes count. When he heard the root crack, he wanted to jump back out of the way, but he forced himself to land a few more strokes for good measure. Then he dropped the axe, put his shoulder under the stump, and heaved. It went. The team strained forward at last, hauling the stump up and out, then stopped, sweating in the rain, their heads down, their muscles twitching and trembling. For the first time in his work with Bert, Arthur saw blood flecks on their backs.

Bert let them rest while Arthur, his knees shaky, hoisted himself out of the crater. Then Bert had the team drag the stump to the side of the clearing with the others, waiting to be burned. Arthur shot a victorious look into the deep, ragged hole —that escapade had shown Bert and made the day end right, with everything done as he'd wanted.

"Come have some coffee before you go," he offered, feeling like Bert's equal for once.

Bert smiled, Arthur thought with approval, but he feared— he always feared—with a trace of amusement, too.

"Had enough of your bad coffee at noon. When you gonna tackle that other little stump?" Bert pointed to the knee high remains, over by the cabin, of the one really giant tree Arthur had had to deal with on his land.

If Arthur could have waved a wand and made that stump disappear, he would have, for though it was something to show off and brag about, it also bothered him. It took up space he wanted. He'd come west to tame a section of the wilderness. That colossal stump reminded him every day that the wilderness might not ever really submit.

"Oh, that one," he replied. "I've decided to let that one stay."

"There'll be stumps for future generations," Bert said.

"Speaking of future generations, how's the new child and the missus?"

"They're doing okay. My wife's still awful tired. The new baby's name is Frieda, after my mother in the old country. She'll be pleased."

Again, Arthur felt a bit in awe of Bert, who was rubbing the sweat from the team as he spoke. The rain had backed off for the moment. It came and went, mostly came. Arthur hadn't realized Bert was still connected to his past, that he had a mother in Germany who was going to like hearing about a namesake granddaughter. As the older man cared for his animals, Arthur saw Bert as the center link of an unbroken family chain that reached backward and forward, even back across the Atlantic. He was aware of his own mother, for whom he would not have named a cat, gladly left behind in Somerville; of his sister in

51

Texas whom he hadn't seen in years; of his father, who had died suddenly and young. Usually he could make his aloneness a sign of strength and independence. But seeing Bert as the tie between his mother back in Europe and his new baby daughter turned Arthur's gravy into gruel.

"My daughter Elva asks me when you're gonna get a housekeeper," Bert said, and Arthur felt as though Bert could look at his face and read his mind. Arthur hadn't planned to tell anyone about Emma's arrival, except maybe Hal Landis, his best friend at the mill. Bert was grinning. Arthur knew Bert had seen how Elva, who was sixteen going on thirty, had been making up to him.

"I'll share Mr. Smollett's hymnal," she'd said when they sang Christmas carols, and she sat next to him whenever he stopped for supper. She ambushed him at Snows' store. Once when he was picking up some books at the post office—one by Mark Twain, a pamphlet on grafting, and a treatise on soils—she'd spied his rectangular package and told him that she'd "read a book once, about a girl who fell in love." She was what his mother would have called "overdeveloped," with sulky blue eyes, cornsilk braids pinned up behind, and a plump, pouty lower lip. When Elva was around, he was hard put to keep in mind the notion he'd been brought up on, that a man's wife should be half his age plus seven—which made Emma, at twenty-five, a better numerical choice.

Emma—why, at this very moment she was on her way—and last night she had disturbed his rest. He'd dreamed that a hat—no face, just a large black woman's hat trimmed with artificial cherries—had appeared outside his window and was trying to get in. He'd woken up, unnerved.

"So—you gonna get a housekeeper and drink decent coffee?" Bert asked again, joshing.

"A housekeeper's on her way," Arthur said. There—let Bert be surprised by that.

"That lady you write to in Vermont?" said Bert, and Arthur realized that it was impossible to surprise anyone in a place the size of North Falls.

"Miss Emma Howe, of Warwick."

Bert nodded, once, as if to say—that's good. "So the local ladies will have broken hearts."

"I guess. If they choose to." Thinking guiltily of some lustful thoughts about Elva, Arthur remembered he hadn't paid Bert and reached for his wallet. After the money had changed hands, Bert clapped him on the back.

"You did good in that hole, Art," he said. "I wouldn't try a stunt like that with just anyone."

Bertram: Bert. Arthur: Art. He liked the sound of it—he'd never had a nickname anywhere back East. His gruel turned back into gravy, at least for a little while.

As Bert clucked to the team and headed toward home, Arthur went into the cabin to stay dry until his hired man, Martin Vogel, came to help with the milking. He held onto that gravy feeling best when he was alone.

VII

At WHITE RIVER JUNCTION, the train stopped for half an hour to add cars, so most of the passengers went into the station to avoid the jolts and bangs. Emma was glad of a chance for some fresh air.

At the refreshment wagon, she met Wilfred's Aunt Emily, trying to carry three cups of cocoa and three buns and keep track of Wilfred and Laura at the same time.

"Let me give you a hand," Emma said, happy for a chance to repay Wilfred's good deed.

"Thank you." Aunt Emily seemed reluctant, yet grateful for Emma's aid. With Emma leading through the crowd, they pushed their way to a bench where they found seats for the children. The steaming cocoa was boiling hot, and in the confusion of the unfamiliar situation, before the little girl could be warned away from her cup, she had eagerly tasted, burned her mouth, and splashed hot brown liquid down the front of her white knitted coat.

Laura's body went rigid. Her eyes looked like stuffed olives and her mouth was a perfect circle of dismay. Then she sucked in an enormous breath and blew it out in a scream that made heads turn. Her eyes squeezed shut. Her lips pulled back from her baby teeth into a grimace and more screams pierced the air. Tears rolled fatly from under her satiny lids.

Something cold—snow! thought Emma instinctively. She ran for the door, scooped up clean handfuls from a windowsill, and raced back to Laura with two soft snowballs.

"Suck on that, quick," she said.

As the wet coldness soothed Laura's injured tongue, her tears stopped. The way Aunt Emily dabbed at the splotch on the white knitted coat made Emma suspect that she had knitted it.

"How *could* you, Laura, when I had you all dressed up? What will Grandmother say?"

"It's not easy, traveling with children," Emma said.

"This trip is especially hard."

"Wilfred told me you're on your way to New York."

"Yes, to leave them with their grandmother, their father's mother."

"You're their aunt?"

"Yes, their mother's sister. I'm Emily Dodge, Mrs. Franklin Dodge. I wish my mother were still alive, so they could go there. My sister Mary. . . ."

Emily Dodge paused, then stepped back from the children. Despite her burned mouth, Laura was comforting herself with her bun—the injury couldn't be so very bad, Emma thought. Wilfred, quietly eating and drinking on the bench, looked up at his aunt's face, then apparently returned his whole attention to his food. Emma recognized something she'd often done herself as a child: on the surface he seemed not to listen to what the grownups said, but he took in every word. His aunt apparently didn't notice his subterfuge, or didn't care about it, for she poured out a torrent of words.

"Mary died after her third baby's birth. Toward the end of the pregnancy, she lost weight instead of gaining and fainted several times. Her ankles swelled and she complained of constant thirst. After the birth, she went into a coma and she never came back. The baby wasn't strong enough to live without her."

"I'm sorry," Emma said, knowing her words were not nearly enough, and that, in fact, Mrs. Dodge was so caught up in her need to tell her story that she couldn't really hear them. Maybe Wilfred would—she hoped so.

"She looked like a girl of nineteen in her casket, tucked up with her favorite doll, for they were buried together, at least. Her pain had been smoothed away, as if it had never happened. The minister said that we were all miserable sinners, that her death was the will of God, that she was happier now, that we must accept God's will because with our imperfect understand-

55

ing we could not comprehend the purpose of His plan. As if a young mother could be 'happier' dead and separated from her children! Her husband beat his fist on the edge of the coffin and cursed heaven. The day after the funeral, he had her clothes and letters burned. Since then, he hasn't seen the children. He won't see them. It's as if they no longer exist for him."

Emma, horrified, didn't know what to say.

"I love them dearly, but my husband says I can't keep them, not with the three we have of our own. So I'm taking them to their father's mother. I *hate* doing it. She's old and stern and deaf. But she's giving them a home. I'll see them when I can. This is their first ride on a train, but the fun of it is spoiled. At my house, they began to smile and play again, but today they seem as they did after Mary died, so sad and serious. With one blow, they lost a loving mother and their father. I blame him. I can't say it to anyone, but I blame him. He's selfish in his grief. He can't see theirs. Instead of comforting each other, everyone's condemned to suffer. I blame my husband, too, but I understand his position and I have to live with him, even if I don't agree with his decision. I don't blame God, because God has changed for me. There is no such thing as 'God's will.' The minister would be shocked. I don't tell him my ideas."

Emma suddenly felt very close to this woman she had known for barely minutes. She, too, had given these matters some thought. Why, she had asked many times, did God make me look the way I do? So plain, so homely. He could have made me pretty just as well. Why? In the course of pondering the answer, Emma's God had become less like a bearded figure in the sky and more like nature itself, which produced tidal waves and rattlesnakes as well as flowers. God could not have *meant* her to be ugly. Well, then, God was without intention.

Through the boredom of winter Sunday school, hungry, her body itchy in woolen underwear, she remembered hearing, from a substitute teacher who must have come in for just that one day, that the Kingdom of Heaven was a pearl of great price. She had looked at her cousin Hannah Walker, in her smocked blue challis dress and high-buttoned boots with her fair hair rippling down her back and tied with a dark blue ribbon. She had thought: So. Cousin Hannah's face was pretty, but it could

56

never be as beautiful as the Kingdom of Heaven because it wasn't struggled for. Emma had read about how a pearl was formed in an oyster because of an irritating speck of sand. It was the result of suffering, and she knew her cousin Hannah had never had to suffer for a thing, certainly not her looks.

In another extraordinary comparison, the same substitute teacher had said that the Kingdom of Heaven was a grain of mustard. Emma had taken this to mean a seed from the mustard plant Pa didn't like to see coming up in his corn. Mustard could take over a field if you weren't careful, for it spread and came back again next year. Actually, Emma had always liked to see its patches of bright yellow on the hillsides. But, at any rate, a grain of mustard was just a common seed. It led to a new plant in the spring, and another new plant after that. Maybe it had grown in the fields Ruth gleaned—it certainly grew in Pa's. And so on, through past and future ages. So the Kingdom of Heaven was . . . it was a struggle to create something beautiful inside you, like the oyster struggling to make the pearl. And it was season after season of mustard growing yellow in the fields and ditches, mustard going on forever from the Begats right down to her there in that stuffy room on that hard chair. *That* was the Kingdom of Heaven, and it was much more difficult and much more ordinary than she had thought!

Now, in the train station, Emma asked Emily Dodge, "And what is your idea of God?" She hoped that perhaps she already knew part of the answer.

"God is not just," Mrs. Dodge replied. "God does not protect the innocent or punish the evildoer. Justice has nothing to do with God. He didn't punish Mary for her sins. I can't accept that and I won't. My sister was *not* a 'miserable sinner,' only ill! She died at thirty-two after a blameless life and she deserved not one stroke of the whip though she received many. Our trials are simply our trials, because that is how life is, and God is *not* in heaven. God is in us. God is our strength and our goodness to each other, which helps us bear the injustice and pain of life. If I didn't *know* that, I couldn't live. I couldn't send these children away, and I couldn't go on living with my husband."

Emma, who had never discussed these matters with another

57

soul, felt tears of agreement well up in her eyes. "You're right about God," she said. "I think that way, too."

"Do you?"

"Yes!"

A secret look of recognition passed between the two.

"Maybe your husband will change his mind and the children will come back to you."

Ushering Laura and Wilfred back toward the train, Emily Dodge shook her head. "I thought I knew my husband before I married him. I thought I could predict his behavior in any situation. But a woman never truly knows a man until it's too late, because a suitor is not the same as a husband. A suitor is all smiles, and wishes, and attentions, and lies. A husband is facts. My husband won't alter." She gave Emma a bitter little smile. "It's a great principle with him never to change his mind—he takes it as a sign of weakness."

They climbed back aboard, Emily carrying Laura and Emma boosting Wilfred once again. As they made their way down the aisle and were again surrounded by the commercial traveler, the man with the flask, the snorer, and Emma's posh but sour seatmate, Mrs. Dodge suddenly turned to Emma with a too-bright smile. In a public tone, she said, "And now you must tell me about *your* trip. Where are *you* going and why are you on the train?"

Emma became anxious about blocking the aisle. She was being carried away from her moment of intimacy with Emily by the crowd, and Emily clearly felt it too and was being drawn back into conventional behavior.

"Visiting," Emma answered, forced by the situation into an answer that concealed and thus was only partly true. "Goodbye," she called, as the press of passengers swept her along and she left Emily Dodge and the children behind.

The day wore on. Emma read, dozed, looked out the window, knitted, ate a hermit, drank some tea, and then did all of those things again. She considered the notion that a suitor was not the same as a husband, that Arthur writing her amusing letters might have some ideas about life that she would not like at all and would not discover until after she had married him. How could she find out—before. Assuming, of course, that he still wanted to marry her after he had seen her. "Beggars can't be choosers," she thought out of habit, and then asserted angrily, "but I'm not a beggar!"

She would wait to see if he wanted her. That would be the hard part, knowing that he might not want her. Paul had, but then Paul had been a foreigner, speaking hardly any English, lonely and away from home. If Arthur did want her, she decided that somehow, she didn't know how exactly, she would put him to the test. She would not get trapped. She would find out about him before it was too late.

Finally at dusk the conductor called out "New York!" and Emma woke instantly from her traveler's doze. Passengers crowded the aisle, hurrying to retrieve their bags and get off. Emma collected her luggage and moved with the flow of people to the platform. Now she had to change stations. Again she joined the human stream and made her way out of the station to the street, where snowflakes fluttered. The city, what she could see of it, was bustling, tall, dirty, and exciting. She was glad she had resisted Aunt Josephine's advice—the only advice she'd offered except that Emma should stay at home—to travel by way of Canada. Getting a glimpse of New York was worth a few extra miles.

As she waited for a hack, Emma saw Wilfred and Emily Dodge walking slowly down the sidewalk away from her, toward a waiting carriage. Snow whirled around them. Emily held Wilfred's hand and carried the exhausted Laura on her shoulder, where her limp arm lolled in rhythm with Emily Dodge's heavy steps.

VIII

ARTHUR LEFT his muddy boots by the door to save his brand new flooring. On the coals in the stove, he laid a split chunk of well-dried pine cut precisely to fit the fire box. He put his stocking feet on a stool by the stove, leaned back in his chair, and closed his eyes, waiting for his bad coffee to heat.

The rain, which would soak the newly cleared land—delaying the underdrain he wanted to install, delaying the plowing, adding to the already generous supply of mud—beat down steadily. In spite of himself, he found the sound of it soothing.

As he rested, Emma crept into his thoughts again. Suppose she were here now. Part of him didn't believe that would really happen. It was as though he had invited her as a kind of dare or joke and she had taken him up on it. But anyway, just suppose. Could they sit together quietly, listening to the rain, hearing the fire crackle, smelling woodsmoke, damp earth, and coffee? Could he sit in this room that he'd built with his two hands and, in a private, inner, wordless place, be *known* by her?

At the sound of boiling, his eyes flew open and he grabbed the pot off the stove. "Boiled coffee is spoiled coffee," his mother used to say in her "I told you so" voice. For years, out of spite, he drank boiled coffee and claimed he liked it. Then one day he tasted it, really tasted it, and realized that of course—damn the woman—she was right. That was part of the trouble with her.

She talked incessantly. Once as a child he'd sneaked out of the room in midsentence. Her narrow back was turned to him, elbows cocked like chicken wings as she wrung out the draggled mesh dishcloth at the long tin sink. Her very apron bow, adroop, had looked angry and misunderstood. He'd tiptoed backwards through the door and down the hall, then heard her high-pitched cry when she realized that she'd been talking on for minutes to an empty room. But often—*damn* the woman—she was right. Boiled coffee wasn't fit to drink and there was no time to make a fresh pot. He poured it, hissing, into the slop bucket, pulled on his boots, and went out to meet Martin Vogel in the barn.

Martin was already milking. Like Bert Brown, he was of German origin though he was Washington born. He was new to Snohomish, having used his inheritance, $150, to buy the relinquishment of a fellow named Thomas to a place not far from Bert's. Thomas had given up his section, a beaten man. As Bert sometimes said, homesteading wasn't for everybody.

When Hal Landis's mill was running, Martin worked there. When the mill was closed, he was Arthur's hired hand. Sometimes he hustled and did both. He picked up work where he could, especially since he'd gotten married, at twenty, just three weeks before.

"Good evening, Martin," Arthur said.

The barn was really just a three-sided shed to keep the hay dry and make a place for milking, but still it was dusky inside and Arthur had to let his eyes adjust.

"Evening, Arthur."

Before his marriage, Martin had called him Mr. Smollett. Arthur felt at ease with Martin—no need, as with Bert, to prove himself. Sometimes, though, he took the joshing position. Did the old just naturally need to tease the young?

"How's everything at home?"

"Annie's fine. She's planning the garden. Sorting the peas and such, got the windowsills full of onions and cabbage."

"You'll have an early start."

"I've been helping her with the fencing."

"Deer thick over your way?" Arthur asked, and felt a twinge of his old self-doubts. Not that Martin was much of a hunter.

Martin moved on to the next cow, while Arthur fetched Daffodil, who was pregnant, a measure of grain.

"Not too bad. Plenty of coons and woodchucks, though. The

61

dog helps. I'm surprised you don't keep a dog, Arthur, with all the vegetables you raise."

Arthur sometimes told people that his lettuce came from lettuce—and from potatoes, carrots, cabbage, peas, beans, mustard greens, beets, spinach, onions, and kale. He also grew blackberries, raspberries, and blueberries, having started with bushes that were volunteers. And gooseberries, currants, rhubarb, and apples. The lumberjacks were fond of pie.

"I had a dog until the fall, when he got sick and disappeared. He was old, so I figured he went off to die."

He realized now that when Tige left, and he thought of a replacement, he'd put it off partly because a dog wasn't so needed in the winter and partly because of Emma. He had thought, somewhere deep in his mind, that he'd ask her to come —eventually. He had thought she might. He had waited to choose a dog. Tige had been a one-man beast, obedient, ugly, and fierce. When he was after a snake or rat, his barks were heard all the way to the Browns'—Bert said the sound carried clear as a bell across the pond. Bert, big as he was, had given Tige a wide berth. Dogs formed their loyalties hard and fast.

"Perhaps you'd like a pup? We'll have some soon. Judy's a good dog, she'll have some fine pups. She's part terrier and she's not afraid of weasels. Gets quite a few woodchucks. But she's friendly enough to people, unless something about them strikes her wrong. An Indian peddler came last week while I was away over to North Falls, and Annie had to shut Judy in the shed because she wouldn't stop worrying the man. She didn't like the looks of that peddler."

"Know who the father dog was?"

"Can't say that I do." Martin's laugh sounded a little embarrassed. "There was quite a crowd in our yard for a few days."

"Perhaps I will take a pup, Martin, after Miss Howe arrives."

"Who's Miss Howe?"

Arthur picked that moment to walk out to the pump for a bucket of water. Let Martin wait a moment for the news. Arthur enjoyed building a little suspense.

"I've invited Miss Emma Howe of Warwick, Vermont, to come for a visit. If things work out, I may soon be in your shoes, a man with a new wife."

There. Now he'd told two people, and the more he said it, the more real it became. It seemed natural to talk to Martin about Emma, and such talk came easy at twilight in the dimness of a barn.

"Well, that's good news!" Despite the shadows, Arthur could see the white of Martin's smile.

"I'll look to you for counsel and advice."

Martin ducked his head shyly, but his fingers, blasting milk into the pail, never missed a beat. For a lanky, raw-boned kid, he had gentle hands and a pleasant voice. Sometimes Arthur heard him singing in the barn, hymns mostly.

"I tell you, nothing matches it for settling a man down. I feel ever so much more—calm-like, now that I have Annie."

"Takes good care of you, does she?"

"She's only sixteen, but she had all those younger brothers and sisters and I swear she knows all there is to know about running a house. She's a fine cook and housekeeper, and I've never worn such clean clothes, not since I was at home."

"I suppose she's in a hurry to be a mother."

"Oh, no, at least not right away. We're both hoping we can go on just as we are for a while. Get the place in shape, get a little ahead. It's a treat to come home and find her waiting with supper on the stove and the floors swept and the bed all spread up. She makes such a fuss over me, Arthur, I swear I'm getting spoiled. She learned to make sauerbraten because she knows I like it. It's a fine thing, being a married man. People treat you with more respect. It don't cost much—she eats like a little bird —and she's pretty and she smells so sweet. Evenings, when she brushes out her hair before the fire—well—" He stopped, confused, having perhaps said too much.

Arthur wondered just how long this idyll would last, but he was honest enough to know that he wanted the same thing, the same adoration, if he could get it. He remembered his glorious vision of the buggy ride with Emma down the center of North Falls. And he also knew that he didn't want what his parents had had, his mother dissatisfied and constantly at him, while his father disappeared into his basement workshop, his newspaper, or the store. The complaining, the nagging, and the silence—

no. And then his father had gone off and left him, up and died, just like that.

"What I mean is, I hope things work out for you, Arthur. I'll clean the tie-up and do the chickens."

"Thank you, Martin." Arthur strained the milk and carried it in the dark up to the spring house. No shortage of cooling springs in Snohomish, he thought, and no shortage of romance in Martin, either, or in a marriage only three weeks old, of a couple so young. It couldn't last. In his case, of course, fifteen years would make a difference. He and Emma would be sensible and avoid the disappointments that came after the honeymoon.

When the milk and eggs were ready for delivery in the morning, with some turnips and dried apples, Arthur threw together a supper of bread, potatoes, cabbage, and a shred of ham. Then he sat down to write a letter he'd been putting off. Now that he'd told Bert and Martin about Emma, he had to write to his sister, Nan, older than he by nine years, the plague and idol of his early years.

When his mother was out, doing her church work or visiting among the neighbors, Nan would read to Arthur, murders from the newspaper, fairy tales to make his flesh creep, "Little Orphan Annie" and "The Highwayman," and "Tyger, Tyger, Burning Bright." She sneaked them into the house, having no taste for the uplifting "cautionary tales for young people" that their mother favored. They gave Arthur nightmares, but he loved them. Then he learned to read himself, and sometimes read so hard it seemed the words jumped off the page and left it blank. As if to say, "Now you're on your own," Nan went off to be "finished," fell in love with Cal, a Harvard freshman, and eloped with him back to Texas, where they both forsook their schooling and tended, instead, Cal's father's oil fields. It hadn't been fair. She'd been sort of a buffer. And then she had left.

She wrote at Christmas and on his birthday. She seemed to be doing fine, or at any rate Cal was. She had three grown sons and a stable of riding horses with complicated names. Unlike Arthur, she returned to Somerville once every summer, "to get out of the Texas heat," visiting their mother and old friends. In her recent Christmas letter, she had said: "I'd be willing to have Mother here, but she won't hear of it as we have no Christian Science down our way and she thinks anyone out of Massachusetts walks on all fours. Her health so far is good, despite Mary Baker Eddy, and there things stand. I think she's actually happier now that we're out of her hair. Some people shouldn't have children. I expect she'll outlast you and me on pure cussedness."

At last he had a piece of news for Nan, more than the felling of another fascinating tree or the clearing of another acre.

Dear Nan, he began, then stopped. What was "dear" about her? As children, if he didn't render instant fealty in all things, she pinched him purple and said in a chilling voice, which rang even now in his ears, that if he tattled, he'd be eaten by a black Freegee with eight rows of teeth living huge and invisible under his bed.

He had only once shown interest in a girl while Nan still lived at home. The scorn of her curled lip, the mockery in her eye—"You want to take *Betsy* to the social? Betsy *Witherspoon?* Ooh, nooo!"—had wilted his hopes like hot wind on a row of radish sprouts. He could see Nan opening his letter and cocking one supercilious eyebrow.

"Cal," she'd call to her gigantic Texan husband. "Arthur, my dumb cluck brother, has done it again. That godforsaken homestead wasn't enough. Now he thinks he's going to marry a spinster from back East, some proper maiden lady, a woman he's never laid eyes on. I bet she isn't even pretty. I bet she looks like a witch. Ain't that just like him? Don't that just take the cake?"

As Arthur jutted out his chin, the joints in his jaw slid and hardened. His handwriting, small already, got even tighter, with its letters drawn precisely up and down:

I am pleased to inform you, dear sister, of my impending marriage to Miss Emma Howe, of Warwick, Vermont. Miss Howe is a poetess, seamstress, and daughter of a Civil War veteran.

His heart, a tricky, vulnerable organ, gave a jump in the middle of his chest. It was *not* a mistake, he told himself. It was not the most stupid, foolish, and deluded thing he'd ever done. It was not going to shatter his peace, keep him eating constant gruel instead of gravy, ruin his life. A woman was like the wilderness and only needed a strong hand to keep her in line. For seven years he'd bulled his way through this swamp. By God, he could bull his way through Emma Howe.

IX

"**I**S THIS place free?"

"It most certainly is—do sit down. Let me introduce myself. I'm Lydia Garratt, Mrs. Rufus Garratt."

The train was cold and there were not many female passengers. After a night's layover, Emma had changed stations again, crossing another big city by cab, from the end of the Pennsylvania Railroad to the start of the Chicago, Milwaukee, and St. Paul. She was just now leaving Chicago. Having rejected seats next to a drunk, a priest, and a sailor, she was relieved to find Mrs. Garratt.

Emma pegged Mrs. Garratt at forty, wondered why she always guessed women's ages but never did the same with men, then realized on closer inspection that she could be off by ten years—Mrs. Garratt was so artfully dressed. Her square jaw, under a purple-plumed hat swathed with dotted veiling, was offset by a full, generous mouth. Her eyebrows arched. A bunch of artificial violets—not the cheap kind that looked wilted even new—gave the collar of her black traveling suit a youthful touch, amid swirls of braid and piping. Her buttons, Emma noted, were jet and cost at least twenty-five cents apiece. Emma was suspicious of her hair color, a wonderful peachy red. It might, or might not, be dyed. At home, Clothilde rinsed her hair with strong tea to "mute" the gray, as she so delicately put it, but of course that was not the same thing at all. *Nature's Friends* had once shown colored prints of azaleas in colors so bright Aunt Josephine called them "brazen." For a good twenty minutes, she had extolled in contrast the modest mountain laurels growing at the corners of the Warwick house. Mrs. Garratt, in her purple hat, with high color in her cheeks, reminded Emma of an azalea, a bush that didn't mind saying, "Look at me!" She made Emma feel quite dowdy to be wearing gray.

"And you are? . . ."

"Miss Emma Howe."

"From? . . ."

"Warwick, Vermont."

"Traveling to? . . ."

"Seattle." It wasn't quite a lie, and it sounded much better than North Falls.

"Seattle! Splendid! I've never been there! I'm on my way to St. Paul—and I've never been there, either, though I'm hoping it has some sort of cultural life and a congenial atmosphere. I'm visiting my daughter who has just moved there from Omaha, where she didn't feel at all at home. She trained as a teacher and takes life so seriously, poor thing. It bothered her terribly that Omaha's librarians, in what she calls their 'benighted wisdom,' labeled *Huckleberry Finn*, one of Mr. Twain's books, 'immoral.' They took it off their shelves."

For once, Emma was grateful for Aunt Josephine's "keeping up," as she called it, her magazine subscriptions and her "lectures" during supper. She sensed a test from Mrs. Garratt, and because of Aunt Josephine, at least she had done the reading. Aunt Josephine was opposed to slavery on principle, but she could take no satisfaction from wearing shoes unless someone else went barefoot. In her view, Mr. Twain was "low and vulgar," Huck and Jim were "not high types," and thus not suited to be the subjects of "literature." Emma hadn't agreed, but in Warwick she had held her tongue. Today she said what she thought.

"I liked it when Huck felt bad for making a fool of Jim—and apologized," she said.

Mrs. Garrett beamed and Emma knew she'd passed. "Miss Howe, I see you're not only a reader, but a reader after my own heart. I suppose we must not judge Omaha only by its librarians, but I hope, for my daughter's sake, that St. Paul has faith in the free exchange of ideas. After my visit, I return to Chicago,

68

which is home. I was hoping for some company, so your being here is delightful. The purpose of your journey is? . . ."

"Visiting."

"Ah. Family?"

"Friends." Emma blushed, having made Arthur into a plural. It was one thing to defy Aunt Josephine's opinion about a book, but another to hide the reason for her trip. She saw, by the look on Mrs. Garratt's face, that she hadn't gotten away with this fib. She might as well have blurted—I'm running three thousand miles after a man to get him to marry me.

"Ah. I'm planning to 'visit friends,' too. I'm sure we both know what 'visiting friends' is all about."

"We do?"

Lydia Garratt smoothed a wisp of startling hair up under her grape-colored hat. "A woman can't take out an advertisement in the papers: Attractive widow, well-to-do and well connected, seeks meeting with similarly situated gentleman, with the object of matrimony. References." Lydia laughed, soft and low, in her throat. "And so, she goes avisiting."

"Oh." How could she be so blatant about it? Emma thought.

"Am I right?"

"Right?"

"Come, come, Miss Howe. Enough Yankee reticence. We're in the Middle West now, where the land is flat and facts are facts. 'Fess up."

"Well," said Emma, embarrassed.

Lydia Garratt, in less than a minute, had made more conversational headway than a Howe family member might accomplish in a week. Aunt Josephine talked at people and never listened. Pa and Clothilde hardly spoke at all, unless you got them alone, when they mostly wanted you to sympathize. Anne criticized, Maggie simpered, and Ma murmured to herself in code. Then, of course, there was poor Roland, who would have loved to talk but had no voice. Emma realized that she, too, had remained silent for the most part, though, like Wilfred on his bench in the railroad station, she'd taken it all in. Maybe that was why she had so loved writing to Arthur. He would ask a question and she would respond. Then she would ask him a question and he would respond. It seemed like playing tennis, a

69

game she'd only read about but which had captured her imagination as being much more fun than croquet. In her letters to Arthur, there was no Ma to derail the topic, no Josephine to interrupt.

"Well," Emma said. "Yes."

"Ah! So now you know the real reason for my visit to my daughter in St. Paul, and I know why you're going to Seattle. Don't be shy about it, Miss Howe. It doesn't do a bit of good—it just wastes time. Men are often disarmed by directness, so long as one isn't *too* direct. I've already had two husbands and would be glad of a third for the sheer fun of it. Are you going to Seattle to visit your fiancé?"

"Sort of." Emma put her hand over her mouth. "Not exactly."

"Never mind," said Lydia Garratt gaily. "You'll be engaged soon, I'm sure, if you wish to be. Don't be doubtful, Miss Howe, and don't put your hand over your mouth. You seek to hide a flaw but only call attention to it. I like your face. You could capture any man with those eyes. And your smile is pleasant when you don't try to conceal it."

No one had ever said anything like this to Emma before. At home, there had been much talk of the Walker teeth and the Howe teeth, as though they were two opposing teams. The first was "very nice," the second was "a shame," and when you were born, you were assigned to one or the other for life. Ma was on the other team. When Freddie Frye had called Emma "Beaver," the best Ma could come up with was, "Your face will catch up with your teeth, Emma, if you can just be patient." She'd been waiting ten years for that to happen, and now Lydia Garratt, a total stranger until half an hour ago, was telling her the magic time might have come. Could that be, that somewhere between the Warwick station and a train car west of Chicago, her face had finally caught up? The idea made her want to laugh, but also want to cry. She mistrusted this assessment, but also treasured it. It was like balm on a sore she'd been protecting all her life.

"Do you really think so?" she asked. She needed to know that Lydia wasn't just being kind.

"I scarcely know you. I'll probably only see you on this train. Why would I lie to you? Be bold and believe me, Miss Howe.

You must be a bold person or you wouldn't be striking out alone for the Washington Territory like some sort of intrepid pioneer."

"State. Washington became the forty-second state on November 11, 1889." Emma just went ahead and said it. At home, she would have kept quiet, knowing Aunt Josephine would slap her down, would have to know more about Washington than she did and tell her so, at length.

"I see you've done your studying." Lydia Garratt smiled, and in her face Emma saw a quality so rare as to be almost unique: dispassionate, unqualified approval. "Excuse me for presuming, Miss Howe, but I'm twenty years older than you, I'm sure—I judge you to be about twenty-five? I'll be bored to tears on this trip if I have nobody to talk to. In an hour, we'll be called to the dining car, where I have a reservation. I have been dreading a lonely supper. Please. May I invite you to join me?"

Emma was about to make an excuse of some kind, out of the training of a lifetime, when Lydia Garratt went on.

"Hush, hush, no objections. No cold scraps wrapped in grubby paper and brought from home. No poke of greasy fried fish and potatoes purchased from the platform vendor and guaranteed to make you sick. When in Rome, do as the Romans. On a train, one dines in the dining car. I'm going to take my beauty rest now, but afterwards I truly hope you'll be my companion at dinner. At least consider it. You *must* rescue me from the tedium of eating alone."

Lydia Garratt unskewered her hat and laid it on her lap like a big purple meringue. The ten-inch, pearl-topped pin she handed over to Emma.

"If some drunk is rude to you while I sleep," she said, "show him the sharp end of that." She reclined the back of her seat, settled herself, and within a half a minute, she had slid into sleep like a hand into a pocket.

Emma, giving Lydia's sleeping face a glance, felt surprised and oddly safe. The Howes slept in their beds, in their rooms, with the doors shut—never in chairs. Lydia, clearly, was different, and Lydia must trust her. Emma noticed that Lydia's arched eyebrows were russet, matching the peachy-red of her hair. *Not* dyed. She decided, then and there, to accept the

71

invitation. Why had she worked so hard at sewing if not to have some money to spend? When thrift rose up in her mind to scold her, she reached over to Lydia's lap and gently removed her hat, placing it like a talisman on her own gray knees. Then she, too, closed her eyes.

The dining car was far more elegant than the Howe farmhouse parlor. The ceiling was wedding cake frosting—all cupids, swags, and rosettes. Maroon velvet swathed the windows, held by brass fittings and rings. Lacy undercurtains kept the night at bay, and cabbage roses bloomed on the carpet. Gaslight sconces cast an intimate light, bright enough to see by, dim enough to hide the worn spots in the upholstery, the odd gravy stain.

They sat at a table for two, though Emma thought there was enough cutlery for ten. I will just do everything Lydia does, she thought, looking nervously at three forks, two knives, and two spoons.

"Thank you for joining me, Miss Howe," said Lydia Garratt graciously. "I'd be miserable alone."

Imitating Lydia, Emma unfolded her double damask dinner napkin, listening to its wealthy, clothy sound—the much-washed napkins at home were as soft and silent as dust. A waiter in black trousers and a short white jacket came to take their order. Emma recognized him from Aunt Josephine's *Harper's Weekly*, which she left in the parlor for the rest of the family after she had read each new issue in her room. This man must be "the Negro waiter," in the illustrations for serialized novels about the South. In Warwick there were no Negroes, only Canucks, and men never waited on table. Men carved, or served the meat onto the plates. Women fetched and carried, in tea rooms, at Grange suppers, at home.

"I'll have oysters, roast beef—medium rare—and, in honor of my friend who is from New England, Boston cream pie," Lydia told the waiter. "Champagne with the oysters, please. What would you like, Miss Howe?"

Sticking bravely to her rule, Emma said, "I'll have the same," and noticed that Lydia looked pleased.

When the waiter had bowed and padded off, Lydia said, "You're very slender, Miss Howe. I hope you enjoy good food?"

Emma nodded, realizing she was, in fact, quite hungry. She thought with longing of a favorite supper at home—salt pork and milk gravy on a steamy baked potato.

"I enjoy it very much," she said. "But I'm made like my father, and he's very thin." How pleasant it was to tell Lydia something neutral about Pa.

Lydia looked around the room appreciatively. "I've had many a fine dinner in dining cars like this. When I married Rufus, in December of '90, we left for our wedding trip to San Francisco on Christmas Day. It's sentimental of me, but I can still remember the menu for Christmas dinner. It contained forty-five separate dishes to choose from, not including the sauces and wines. Rufus and I counted them."

"Nobody could eat all that," Emma said.

"But we certainly did that dinner justice. It was one of the happiest days of my life. But this is a good day, too. Sometimes it's a relief not to have men around. At least we don't have to discuss Panama, which seems to go on forever. Today's paper said there's more yellow fever there, and many fear the Canal will never be done. Rufus, who was in steel, used to talk a good bit about open and closed shops. That wasn't my favorite topic, either."

Emma could tell that open shops were not what they sounded like, places where a person could buy between six and six. "I read an article this morning," she said, anxious to hold up her end with a tidbit that had caught her eye. "It said a new baby's footprints could be taken by a doctor with lamp soot mixed with syrup. In a tenement. If there was no ink. To identify the baby for life."

Fortunately, since she had nowhere to go with that dead-end item, the waiter came and set down the oysters with a flourish. Despite the motion of the train, he poured the champagne without spilling a drop. Emma noted with horror that the gray, wet blobs before her were raw.

Lydia picked up her glass. "My first marriage was not a success, Miss Howe—more of that later—I have much good advice for you. Have you read *Karezza or The Ethics of Marriage* by Ellen Kay? She argues that our sexual feelings are *not* degrading—an enlightened view. But my second was a triumph. Will

73

you join me in a toast to the memory of my darling Rufus? I hope he's watching us from heaven, or wherever he may be, and delighting in our every bite."

Emma sat quite still, watching the bubbles rise in her tall, conical glass, in a liquid of palest yellow. All she could think of was dandelion wine and Pa. Guilt over defying him was swiftly followed by guilt over breaking the Temperance Pledge, even though she had signed it ten years before. A pledge was a pledge. Dandelion wine hadn't counted since she'd drunk it with Pa at home. Champagne was a true alcoholic beverage.

Lydia Garratt set down the glass she had raised but kept the stem between her fingers. "Miss Howe," she said, "let's be friends. Let's be Emma and Lydia. Let me tell you something I've observed. Many people, women in particular, cry out before they've been hurt. They say 'no' before they've had a chance to consider 'yes.' They reject new things before they have any understanding of what they might be. They're like the baby who lisps, 'I hate peas,' without ever having tried them. A civilized adult woman must not say, 'I don't drink champagne,' never having tried the tiniest sip."

"I'm afraid it will make me drunk."

"Not if you try only a little, slowly, eating food at the same time. The French, a people who rightfully boast of their art, literature, government, and cuisine, have been making and drinking champagne for centuries. Unlike America, France is a great power in the world, respected everywhere. Its history and tradition reach back before Rome—but I don't mean to tell you what you already know. Only about champagne, which perhaps you don't know. It is sun and grapes. It is ease and conversation among friends. It is summer in a glass."

Lydia tilted her head to one side and forward, making her square jaw quite a winning feature. "We're citizens of the world, Emma. Try some champagne, in honor of Rufus Garratt, who so loved a gracious meal, a fine wine, and the company of bright, handsome, adventurous women." She raised her glass.

Emma thought of the many times when Ma had cautioned her, but Pa, by saying nothing or giving her a nod, had urged her on. Sliding down the big hill, up the jump the boys had built over the stone wall, and on down by the big lethal oak, she'd had to steer her wooden runners hard and use her feet as well. She had been scared, but she had done it, and she had climbed the slippery hill to do it again.

One sip, for Mr. Garratt. Lydia touched her glass and the crystal rang. Bubbles went up Emma's nose and she coughed, but the taste was interesting, somewhere in the narrow band between sweet and not sweet at all.

Lydia forked up an oyster, popped it into her ample mouth, and swallowed it down, scarcely seeming to chew. She took a sip of champagne—there must be a trick to it—the bubbles didn't bother her nose. The oyster didn't make her gag or throw up.

Emma poked an oyster with the two-tined fork, since that was what Lydia had used, trying to concentrate on the appealing smell and ignore the slime. When she had it halfway to her lips, it dropped off and slithered onto the tablecloth. Lydia seemed not to notice. Determined to get the pesky object out of sight, Emma gave it a good jab, transported it to her mouth, chewed once and swallowed fast, as though she were taking medicine. How slippery it was, rubbery, salty—alive! She'd seen pictures of the sea and memorized in school, "Roll on, thou deep and dark blue ocean, roll./Ten thousand ships sweep over thee in vain." Sea. Food. I've just eaten seafood, she thought. Being careful not to inhale, she took another tiny sip of champagne without coughing.

X

CARRYING AN unlit lantern, Arthur Smollett swung along the trail to meet Hal Landis at the mill. Then the two of them would go to North Falls for the installation of officers in the Odd Fellows' Hall. It was to be quite an affair: the twenty brothers, the lodge decked out, eighty invited guests, supper afterwards. Arthur was to be the new secretary and Hal the new treasurer. The bachelors, like Arthur, provided money for the supper, and the married men's wives provided most of the food. Hal wasn't married, but his name was on the food list because he lived with his sister Martha, a widow, who prided herself on her cooking.

For the occasion, Arthur wore his hat, his good pants, and an outdoor jacket of dark brown shaggy wool. He didn't own a suit. He was freshly shaved, had trimmed his moustache, and smelled of soap. Under his shirt collar he had tied a narrow plaid scarf of beige, royal blue, and maroon taffeta. It felt unfamiliar around his neck, and he fingered it, wishing the bow had more perk. Even new taffeta went limp in the North Falls climate. He'd heard Martha Landis complain that ginger snaps came crisp from the oven and sagged in half an hour.

The trail and Smollett Creek parted company where the logging road joined the creek and both meandered to the foot of the valley. At that point, the trail cut up the ridge, moving gradually onto firmer ground. He knew every root and stone, every log to be stepped over. As he moved uphill, the air cooled. Some yellow-headed blackbirds in a stand of bare-branched alder gave their last chirring concert of the day. This was his

76

least used trail and he hadn't hacked it back lately. Drops splatted from the trees onto his hat and shoulders. Wet brush smacked against his trousers, and a leafless catbriar tendril grazed his forehead and sank its claws into the tender skin next to his eye, leaving a scratch and a bloody little drip.

"You have to beat it back with a stick." That was what Hal Landis had told Arthur about the wilderness the first day Arthur had set foot in Snohomish County, and that was what ranchers still said today. The trees and underbrush ringing his valley were a constant pressure, always contriving to reclaim his tear-shaped, 160-acre strip. Vines sent out runners. Black raspberry canes, as lavender as a bruise, tipped to the ground and rose fresh from the point of contact, in a continual state of march. Conifers and hardwoods seeded themselves along the borders of his land, and the big cut stumps sent up suckers the size of ordinary trees. "You can't clear and be done," Hal had told him at their first meeting. "You have to keep clearing, just to stay in one place."

When Arthur had gotten off the train in Everett and stood next to his pile of gear to get his bearings, feeling excited, curious, and alone, Hal, big and bearlike, had come lumbering over. Arthur could tell where he'd come from; his shoulders, moustache, and overalls were powdered with sawdust that he had only partly brushed off. There was no train to North Falls in those days, the spur not having been put in. Indeed, there wasn't even a road, which was why Hal Landis was meeting every train with a notebook and a pen. Round-shouldered and soft-bellied, he shambled up to Arthur and towered over him, as pokable as a heap of mashed potatoes.

"How do," he'd said, lifting and replacing his hat, which had one drift of sawdust across the crown and another circling its brim. "You look like a homesteader, sign here if you want the county to throw up a road from Everett to North Falls, I'm Harold Landis, by the way, call me Hal, and you can see that I'm a little bit crazy but you look a little bit crazy, too, or else what would you be doing here spang in the middle of the wilderness, huh?"

Disarmed and charmed, Arthur had signed. The big man

77

read Arthur's signature and thrust out a strong hand. The soft, loose look of him was deceptive.

"How do, Arthur Smollett," he'd said. "Take a pamphlet about the Odd Fellows' Lodge, odd fellows are the only kind of fellows allowed in these parts, an announcement of when the Methodists hold church, a description of the Grange, that about does it. I'm packing up my dog and pony act and taking some supper at the Everett Inn, it's a good place, which is lucky since it's the only place, come along and be company."

He'd picked up the two boxes of tools—Arthur's heaviest luggage—and led him away, like a rough-coated Newfoundland dog leading a small, neat border collie. Both were twenty-eight years old. Hal's family were some of the original North Falls settlers. Haskell and Inez Landis—Hal's parents—introduced Arthur around, gave advice, invited him to supper. He and Hal had been friends ever since.

Neither had had much time to spare. Arthur was clearing his land and usually working two jobs, or putting in a long, hard stint at a lumber camp. But Hal and Arthur "ran together" those first few years. They learned surveying. They worked on the gang that built the plank road between Everett and North Falls when the county finally allocated the funds. They threw a party to celebrate Haskell and Inez's thirtieth wedding anniversary, and then went out for a private celebration of bachelorhood. They went fishing for trout and salmon. Arthur discovered he liked to fish.

Hal had taken Arthur hunting, too, after which Arthur knew he didn't like to hunt. He hated the feeling of shame he had when Hal got his buck, as though Arthur should apologize to the deer because they'd killed it and to Hal because he, Arthur, hadn't killed one, hadn't taken a shot all day, hadn't wanted to, even though he'd had the chance. The truth was he was afraid to. He disliked himself for being afraid and he certainly couldn't tell Hal about it.

The hunting trip had made them both so uncomfortable that they'd hung the dripping carcass at the mill and gone drinking in Everett. Getting comfortable required two whiskeys for Arthur and four for Hal. Then Hal insisted that they move on to Betty Pilchuck's, where he had some more whiskey, bragged about his prowess as a hunter, kissed Betty, ragged Arthur about his failure of manhood almost to the point of a fight, and passed out.

At that point in the evening, Arthur had been feeling pretty desperate, and Betty had given him a look that said—all right. She was a short, chunky half-breed, a few years younger than he, though at that point he was past judging—she could have been fifteen or fifty, for all he knew. She raised a few chickens and ran her bar with its famous back room. Her father had been a Swede who'd boiled his brains on poison home-still liquor and then laid himself down on the railroad tracks in front of an oncoming train, on purpose or by chance, nobody knew. The locomotive engineer, when he realized what his train had hit, drowned himself a month afterwards. Betty grew up with her mother the best way she could, in the no-man's-land between the growing settlement of whites and what was left of the Chinooks.

When Arthur had gone to her dark room behind the bar, he wanted something hard and quick, like the shooting of the deer, and that was what he got. Betty was like his first woman, a Jamaican who met every ship, including his when it docked to load bananas and he'd known by the palm trees and the heat that he had finally gotten away from Somerville, Massachusetts. But Betty, at least, didn't curse him and throw him out afterwards, as he'd been warned would happen by a shipmate, and which did. He'd slept the night with Betty Pilchuck curled against his back like a small, warm animal. The next day, when Arthur signed on for another three months of hard labor in the lumber camps, he and Hal had parted just about even. They'd never mentioned Betty or the hunting trip again.

Then Haskell died, and Hal had taken over the mill. Hal's sister Martha had been left a widow with five little babies when her husband hit himself in the shin with an axe and got a case of blood poisoning. Martha moved back to the mill with her brood. Suddenly Hal was heading not only the mill but a household comprised of his mother, his sister, and five nieces and nephews. Hal and Arthur joined the Odd Fellows. Hal, seeming to need divine assistance with his new responsibilities, even went so far as to be sprinkled and become a Methodist. They were no

79

longer the young men of the county. They were on their way to pillardom. Hal grew a beard.

Fingering his own smooth-shaven chin, Arthur paused at the narrow top of the ridge to look back, as he always did, and survey his land. At this spot where the trees stood like sentinels along the opposing ridge, he often remembered one of his mother's poetic moments. He'd asked her, as a child at bedtime before they'd had their never-mended rift—"Why are there trees?" She had looked out the window where night was falling and said— "Why, to prop up the darkness." Her words had been just the right ones for him. They'd fallen into his brain like coins into a pig bank.

Here at the boundary line of his property, he felt, always, a dilution. In his domain below, now a stretch of foggy darkness though light still tipped the treetops on the other side, his powers gathered and deepened like water in a pool. When he left his ranch, the gatheredness leaked away. Much as he liked a trip to town, an evening with the Browns or Hal and Martha, he felt most himself on his own land, even though he had a private sense that it wasn't really his. Like the whole nation, it had been stolen from the Indians. Besides, nobody could really "own" land. He was just the caretaker of the moment, and if he was lucky enough to have children, it wouldn't be "theirs," either, except as a kind of long-term loan. The day he finally felled his one gigantic tree whose stump still remained, after days of chopping, sawing, and wedging, after the *boom* and the bounce and the settling of the cracked bundle of branches, he had lain down in the dirt and wood chips beside it and let the rain fall into his face. He'd seen the individual drops, gray on gray against the sky, move toward him just before they landed in his eyes. He'd closed his lids and let the rain fall.

He turned now and followed the downward path toward the light in Hal's kitchen, planting his boots carefully on the slippery slope, feeling the pull on his knees as they braked him.

Hal's niece, Lillian, six years old and so finely blond her hair seemed like wisps of white flame, was posted on the porch, guarding the two food baskets and watching for him. Rusty, the mill-yard dog, heard him first and barked over by the smoking charcoal maker and the sheds. When Arthur emerged from the trees into the clearing around the house, Lillian called out to quiet Rusty and darted inside like a startled partridge. "Uncle Hal!" Arthur heard her pipe, "Mr. Smollett's here!"

Hal appeared in the doorway, a tall, dark form in a shaft of light, pulling on his jacket. Lillian peeked around the doorjamb and Arthur waved to her.

"You put me in mind of your father there a minute," Arthur said to Hal. Haskell Landis had been a big man, too, though he had shriveled some toward the end.

"It's his coat. He told Ma it was too good for his funeral, she took that to mean that I should have it, so we buried him in a tailcoat of Grandpa's from the attic. Pa didn't look like himself in it, but then, who does, dead?" Hal chuckled and handed Arthur a hamper.

"You got bricks in this?"

"Don't let Martha hear you, you know how vain she is about her airy crust, she's been teaching Lillian and I hear her saying, over and over, 'It's got to be light as a feather, it should melt away in the mouth,' the hampers are heavy 'cause they've got plates in the bottom."

Hal lit his and Arthur's lanterns and they set off down the road. As the lanterns swayed, their shadows stretched and shrank, stretched and shrank. It was cooler now, nearly full dark, and the air was drier.

"Might clear up later," Arthur said. He smelled the damp forest, kerosene, and rolling up out of the hampers like a beckoning hand, fruit and spice: pumpkin and mince.

"Got your part learned?" Hal asked.

"It's not much."

"Nor mine, I say my treasurer's vow, and then it's all 'Repeat after me,' I'm in no hurry to reach my Third Degree, all those speeches to get by heart."

"It'll be a fine occasion, though."

The Odd Fellows filled a gap in Arthur's life. He couldn't say much for the banners that would be hung over the stage, reminding the brothers of mortality with a skull and crossbones and of the all-knowingness of God through a single eye. The first made him think of pirates, and the second reminded him of the sign hung out by an enterprising optometrist in Boston whose

81

office he used to pass. But he liked the three links that stood for friendship, love, and truth, and the quiet way the brothers had of pitching in when there was trouble. He liked, in small doses, mingling with the other men.

"I'm proud to be a member," Hal said. "The Odd Fellows did a lot after the Seattle fire. I remember my relatives telling about it."

"Been down that way?"

"Went down with a load of lumber last week, a first-time customer, so I thought I would, it's a new city, Arthur, ever since that Yukon gold came in, it's changed so I hardly know it, it was a sleepy little port, now it's a boom town, the outfitters are making out the best, but everybody's profiting, in Pa's day Seattle orders were rare as hen's teeth, but there's building all over town and we stand to gain by it, now we've got the train, you haven't been in a while?"

"Not lately. I don't much like it."

"You ought to take a look, my cousin has a cannery, and is doing that well, he's talking about buying himself a Ford, soon as they're available, he's been hearing about them in the papers, and don't you know, if there's any new gadget to be had, he must have one."

That could be as much as $400! Arthur thought, maybe more. "If there's no gold, there's always fish," he said.

"That's it, it makes me chafe a bit, living here."

"You'd like to move?" The idea was so foreign to Arthur as to be almost unthinkable.

"Ma wouldn't hear of it, and of course Martha won't budge, but yes, if Martha remarried and I were free to go. . . ." Hal threw Arthur a meaningful look.

Arthur ignored it, as he had ignored other such hints from Hal, though Hal was a hard man to ignore—sort of like ignoring a boulder that had dropped on your foot.

"Think McBride'll run again?" Arthur said.

"Probably not, he's been better than that Rogers, though, Pa always said you could tell a Democrat governor by the free way he'd spend other people's money and by his empty pockets."

"You can have my share of Seattle and welcome to it. The air's not fit to breathe."

82

"I admit there's an occasional stink of fish guts and a press of people on the street, but I like that, you know what I make like sometimes? I make like Martha remarries, a steady sort, someone who'll run the business and be a father to all those kids of hers, then I take Betty Pilchuck and go live in Seattle."

"No!" Arthur stopped in his tracks for half a beat.

"Why not?" Hal laughed.

"Did you ever go there again?"

"Yes, I do."

"You sly dog. I should have known. And you'd marry Betty, no matter?"

"I would, she's not that way anymore."

"An Indian!" But what he was really thinking was—a whore. He'd never want as a wife a woman other men had had, or a woman who'd held herself that low.

"Half, the Chinooks are clever enough, everyone's entitled to their own mistakes, Arthur, why some folks invite maiden ladies from Vermont to come to supper, when there's healthy young widows right over the ridge, of solid family, where they could be part of a business and do right smart."

"You've heard, then. I was set to let you know tonight."

"Martin told me."

"You think I've parted company with my senses?"

"Oh, not as bad as that, I'm sure we'll all take to Miss Howe, once we get used to her, I know you never fancied Martha and her tribe of young ones, this is just talk, Arthur, I know with you I'm free to talk, you're not the only one hankering after a change."

"Martha's a good woman."

Hal snorted. "Of course she is, though she didn't show much judgment when she picked Roy Ward to marry, anyone but Martha would have known he was bound to chop himself in the leg or some other foolishness, fall down in a mine shaft, drown in a well, Pa wouldn't let Roy near the saws, said he didn't want anything on his conscience, with some folks it's just a matter of time, Martha always was bringing home birds with broken wings."

"She's a fine mother."

"Yes, she's in her element, half mother Earth, half drill sergeant, has a real sense of family, too, look at their names: Roy, Jr., for his dad, even if he was a jackass, Haskell for Pa and Harold for me, Cora and Lillian for Roy's two grandmothers."

Arthur wasn't sure he should say what was on his mind, but he went ahead.

"That's why I never fancied her, though it's selfish of me. I want my own children. I want my own flesh and blood on the ranch. And I want—don't laugh now—I want their mother to be the sort of person who can see the beauty in a cut cabbage." There was more he didn't say—that he didn't want to start out being a lover to a woman who'd be measuring him against husband number one, even if it was only Roy Ward. Five children—he must not have been that bad.

"Spoken like a farmer, I've always thought cabbages were mighty—cute, sure you don't want to marry me?"

Arthur gave Hal a punch in the arm and Hal laughed.

"You always were stubborn, Arthur, have to have things your own mulish way, I say, these baskets are heavy, let's lighten our load a bit and eat one of the pies, just another way to carry it."

Arthur smiled. This was the Hal he knew and loved. "You think we should?"

"I think we will, should or no, I'm partial to rhubarb myself, but since it's not available I'll settle for mince, it's a long time since dinner." The lanterns made two pools of yellow light. Hal squatted at the roadside and divided the pie with a pocket knife, then quartered it and cut the quarters again. He ate an eighth in one bite.

"Good pie," said Arthur, with his mouth full.

"Never tastes as good at the table."

In five minutes, it was gone. They wandered into the weeds away from the road and unbottoned. The hemlock branches in front of them were covered with cones. The urine hissed against the tree's bark, and their streams mingled, a reminder to Arthur of old times, a sign that they wouldn't repeat their talk to others. They shook themselves dry, tucked in, buttoned up. In the top of the hemlock, an owl hooted.

"Well," said Hal, "that's better."

XI

AFTER HER dinner with Lydia, Emma slept in a Pullman berth, but it turned out to be an upper and not exactly restful. The modesty of female passengers was protected by giving them chin-to-toe Pullman coats to undress beneath. Her gray traveling dress, whose hem was gritty with the dirt of many days, had fifteen tiny buttons in groups of three, and a placket at the side closed by hooks and eyes. Her cuffs had six buttons each. Her skirt, which brushed her shoe tops, contained four yards of gray woolen worsted. The dress would come off only over her head, a fact she recalled only after perspiring through the placket and the twenty-seven buttons under the five-pound Pullman coat. The only advantage to the berth was being able to lie flat for the first time in days, her bones sharp on the skimpy mattress, her head on a wafer of pillow. Still, her feet tingled with relief and the ache in her back began to fade. But the train's motion edged her first against the cold outer wall of the berth, then toward the abyss below the edge. All night she felt at risk and woke up sore all over from keeping her muscles tensed for the crash even as she dozed.

The next morning Emma said good-bye to Lydia, and then the train began crossing, crossing, crossing the plains, on the tracks of the Great Northern Railway. At first Emma was fascinated by the enormous sky and endless sweeps of space. But the vast snow-blown emptiness soon became daunting, and the novelty of travel had long since palled. Now, on another endless afternoon, she tried to make her body easeful, turning from side to side on the unyielding contours of the seat. Her eyes were half closed; she didn't bother to peer out the window. She'd lost track of how long she had been on the train—it seemed like always.

Most of the other passengers were also too bored to look out the window and too exhausted to complain. The train clacked and swayed. The slanting sun assaulted them, did violence to their eyes, brought on migraine. The toilet smelled. The dining and Pullman cars were gone now—everyone slept uncomfortably and democratically in the coach. At irregular intervals, sketchy meals could be bought at local stops, but they were often left unfinished for lack of time. Emma thought she'd die happy if she never saw another boiled bean. She had long since given up on conversation and on being "usefully employed"— reading, knitting, writing. She couldn't summon the will to make the effort. She needed no mirror to tell her there were circles beneath her eyes and that her unbrushed, unwashed hair looked greasy. A blind pimple forming on her chin radiated little stabs of pain when she rubbed it with her finger. She felt parched, limp, and constipated. She yearned for a crisp apple and lemonade.

By five o'clock the passengers gave in completely to stupor and the car was dull and still. The colicky baby that had gotten on with its mother at midday and cried for most of the afternoon in a pitiful, whiny mew, wore itself out and fell asleep. A ragged, bearded man had joined them humming in Minot, North Dakota. He lugged a burlap bag of turnips, a shotgun, and a dead turkey. Now he sat unwinding a dirty bandage from his thumb, dropped the soiled cloth in the aisle, and sat staring quietly at his raw, unscabbed gash. The lovers who had boarded in Fargo, the wall-eyed boy and the girl scarred as if by a knife along one cheek, ran out of bakery endearments—no more "sugar cookie," "honey bun," "molasses pie." They lay entwined but silent.

At six, the train stopped briefly for mail. People hurried to the station to buy supper. The evening dragged, despite card games and some singing. The night was long, punctuated by coughs, snoring, and the passing of gas. Emma's aching joints and dry throat gave rise to garish dreams that woke her with no memory of their content. When the dark was blackest, she heard eerie mutters and one strange, incoherent cry. The ragged, bearded man needing the toilet often riled those sleeping near him with his frequent trips and fumbling in the dark.

Dawn was a blessing. People roused and tidied themselves. They bought food from vendors walking the aisles with their baskets. Over rolls and coffee, people talked quietly, commiserating about the rigors of travel, looking forward to getting off as to getting out of jail. The mood was cheerful, and the girl with the scar reached into her private stores and shared with Emma the blackberry jam she'd brought from home.

But the well-being of morning was brief and quickly faded into the exhaustion of another afternoon and the vain attempt at rest during another night. Emma's every cell yearned to lie down alone in a dark, quiet, unmoving place for a long, long time. The train's motion moved from the wheels through the struts and joists directly into her bones, which seemed to have turned to jelly on purpose to absorb it. She thought with longing of her room at home and the watchful, unmoving elm outside her window.

Around two A.M. she dropped into sleep at last along with most of the other riders, only to be woken by a bump in her back. She heard panting and wrestling. She thought someone was in trouble, perhaps struggling with a thief, till she heard a young man's voice murmur a thick endearment and the girl with the scar reply. The couple that boarded in Denver—they were making love in the seat behind her.

At first she tensed all over, dumbfounded and offended. Some people, she thought, have no shame. Then she remembered how Pa had announced one morning when she was twelve and all ears, "The heifer's just about ripe. Needs the bull the way a woman needs a man." Ma's mouth had pleated up with disapproval like a folded paper fan. "Human beings have no animal nature," she had asserted. Pa had smiled quizzically at the fat sugar bowl. "That's as it may be," he'd said, and Emma had filed away the meaning of that smile.

When Paul had come, a lonely foreigner, to help with the hay, she'd been strongly drawn to his dark curly hair, his skin that quickly tanned, his gesturing hands and strong, narrow shoulders. She liked his laugh—even it sounded French to her. What was more wonderful was that he'd reached out to her from his alien's position and recognized that this skinny girl, who followed behind the wagon with her rake to get up the last bits, was also alone despite two sisters, parents, aunts, a hired man, and a cat. He had kissed a mouth she'd thought nobody wanted. His hands had touched her in places that had made her feel ashamed, and he'd kept touching her until the shame gave way to desire. He had taught her to touch him. *C'est ça, c'est ça,* he'd whisper in the wooded dark where they met, and cry aloud softly when it was over.

So she had no right to be offended, and when she lay back in her seat, the tension gone, she felt a swelling softness between her thighs, something she had not felt in a long time. She was so tired. She had no energy to judge that couple wrong, even though she now could see the girl's foot in its black cotton stocking push itself into the space between the seat and the window not a yard away.

Indeed, as the bumps in Emma's back quickened, and finally she heard an ultimate moan and watched, mesmerized, as the toes inside the stocking curled, she realized something she had never known before. That last night of the summer, at the French Canadians' barn dance, the night before Paul went back to Quebec, he'd wanted to be inside her with more than just his fingers. She had been afraid—she didn't want to be left with a baby and she didn't want to face Pa. But she should have let him. As it turned out, Pa had assumed the worst anyway so she might as well have. From the vantage point of the train, she looked back on that fearful girl of nineteen and knew—I should have let him. She felt now on the train the same emptiness, the yearning, the loneliness she had struggled with after Paul went away. It was part of the reason she was going to North Falls.

She slept. She woke in the early morning with the sun behind her, lighting up snow-covered crags so overwhelming in their size, beauty, and grandeur that she gasped out loud.

The conductor, who happened to be passing by at that moment, looked down at her and smiled.

"That's them," he said. "Those are the Rockies."

88

XII

FROM A distance, the Odd Fellows' Hall glowed like a lighted jack-o'-lantern at the foot of the dark hill. As yet the building was unpainted—funds had barely paid for the roof, never mind cosmetic frills—but the wood still had a clean look. The night was cold enough so it didn't seem to matter that most of the windows were swollen shut, or that the doors were sticking in their jambs. The people gathering outside seemed eager for tonight's festivities. It wasn't often that guests were invited to witness the rituals inside.

"At last, Martha Ward's pies!" cried Madge Parsons, loud as a hog caller as she spotted Arthur and Hal. She was an officer of the sister group, the Rebekahs, a woman with a shelf of bosom balanced by a shelf of rear.

"Where've you been so long, Harold Landis? You must have loitered on the way."

"Evening, Madge," said Hal equitably. "I'll be glad to turn these hampers over to you, but I want a receipt."

Madge smiled and shook her fist at him. "You, Bill," she called and her half-grown son unfolded himself like a jackknife from the porch steps and carried the baskets away.

"We're about to begin," the master of ceremonies, Jason Parsons, told Hal and Arthur. He was a Jack Sprat to his wife, his slender build accentuated by large dark eyes, a bony face, and a long narrow nose. His moustache and bushy eyebrows had authority.

"Time to come in!" Parsons called to the children playing tag under the trees. "Just starting, folks," he announced to the small

89

groups gathered to chat in the yard. Arthur saw the numerous Browns, including Dee and the new baby, scrubbed and polished, driving up in their crowded wagon. Bert was wearing his store teeth for the occasion. Arthur avoided meeting Elva's eye. "We'll go in through the back," Mr. Parsons told Hal and Arthur. He led them around the side entrance to the small backstage antechamber. Other members arrived, exchanged greetings, removed their hats, coughed, and shuffled their feet. Hal combed his fingers through his beard. Arthur adjusted his drooping tie. He remembered, for some reason, the evening when he and Ben Jones, aged twelve, were supposed to join the church back in Somerville, twenty years ago, but had scandalized everyone and humiliated themselves by not going forward when they were called. It had been planned as a joke but had backfired. He wished now he were somewhere else, on midnight watch in a hurricane, maybe, or fighting a brushfire.

Jason Parsons fussed over the tray of seals and ribbons and over the order of ceremonies, in a leather-bound book. The little room was airless, with a lamp burning and a dead bouquet from last summer, brittle in a vase on the shelf. At last Mr. Parsons was satisfied and they filed out to the stage in solemn procession, as though they were entering a morgue to identify a body.

Arthur was struck by the noise, the vastness of the room, and the many, many faces. One hundred people in the same room all at one time!—his heart thumped in his chest and his palms grew moist. At first he could only see eyes, like the single all-knowing eye of God, over and over. Then he identified Martin Vogel smiling at him from the front row and calmed down. There were the Browns, Elva in blue polka dots, taking seats in the back, probably in case Dee had to slip out with the baby.

There was no piano, thank goodness. The Odd Fellows' Hall in Everett had one, a Beckwith Home Favorite with Mandolin Attachment, $89 new. After a year of damp, mildew, and disuse, it had popped most of its ivories and was so out of tune it would make a saint shudder. So Harry Snow, who'd driven tonight in his new buggy even though it was only five hundred yards, stepped forward as master of music. He peeped a pitch pipe and led off in a vibrating tenor. Arthur had played the piano once, taught briefly by his mother, and he liked the tune of "Rock of Ages." He enjoyed singing a hymn now and again, so long as he didn't have to embrace its creed. When Amos Brill got up to deliver the prayer, Arthur didn't bow his head more than an inch or two, but he was happy to close his eyes and indulge in some quiet meditation.

Once things were off to a good start, Arthur didn't mind the ceremony, the reports, the speeches, readings, and songs. As he ducked his head to receive the secretary's seal and ribbon, he felt himself a North Falls citizen in good standing. How much more a part of things he would feel as a married man. Nearly all of the Odd Fellows were married. There was something public about marriage that pleased him. He looked out into the audience, thinking, won't they be surprised! But, he thought, no such show as this—oh, no! A line or two in the Everett newspaper, that would suffice. A public announcement of a private vow.

The confident set of his head altered after he bowed it again in the antechamber so Jason Parsons could put away the ribbons. Back to normal, he moved with the brothers into the hall where now the chairs were being scraped back and the tables hauled out. Sooner or later this evening, as sure as God put worms in apples, he would have to face Elva Brown.

It didn't happen right away, and for a while he thought he'd gotten off, come to school without his lesson learned and not been called on by the teacher. The plank tables laid on sawhorses and covered with white paper were spread with food, and though still quite full of pie, he helped himself to beans baked with salt pork, corn pudding, slaw, and coffee.

"Evening, Mr. Secretary," Martin Vogel called. "Come sit."

"How do, Martin."

"So many people," Annie said admiringly.

"A good show," said Arthur. "How's everything up your way?"

Martin said, "Judy had her puppies. Five of them, three spotted and two mostly black. You're welcome to take one soon as they're weaned."

"It could be a present for the Miss Howe I've heard about," said Annie, smiling.

"A farm dog's not a lap dog, Annie," admonished Martin.

"But Miss Howe will be refined," Annie said, "with a picture hat and trimming on her cuffs. An Eastern lady and delicate, ain't that right, Arthur? I've seen photos of Eastern ladies and they often carry a little dog under one arm, like a toy. Dress them in jewels and little coats, they do."

"Miss Howe is a farm girl, Annie, no more refined than you," said Arthur. "At least she'd better not be."

"Oh, dear. Well, all the better. I look forward to a woman neighbor."

Annie colored and Martin looked flustered, too. "Seems we're expecting," he said with more than a little melancholy. The honeymoon was over.

Arthur did a rapid calculation or two and reckoned that this baby had gone with Annie to the preacher.

"So soon! Well, that's fine news. Good luck to you both."

"Things change so fast," said Annie. "You just get used to one way and another comes along. But we're pleased. Aren't we, Martin?"

"Yes, indeed." Martin swallowed with a little audible click. Arthur, watching his Adam's apple bob up and down, hoped that Martin had no doubts about who this father dog might be.

"The whole area's growing by leaps and bounds," Arthur said to fill in the awkward silence. "Hal Landis tells me you can't find room to stand on the streets of Seattle. Look how North Falls has grown, since I came here seven years ago. You're part of that expansion, Martin, you and your family. Snohomish County's doing its part. America's growing and we're growing with it."

"Growing up, I guess you mean," said Martin.

"That's about it. Our Revolution made us a child nation, and then we struggled out of short pants when we had our Civil War. Now we're coming of age."

Annie stifled a yawn. "Well, we wish you well, Arthur, with Miss Howe, I mean. Is she very beautiful?"

Arthur looked across the dirty plates at the pretty face opposite him. There wasn't a flaw in it, and her brown eyes were shining under her wavy brown bangs. She couldn't have played Martin false or tricked him—could she?

"She's not beautiful at all when compared to present com-

92

pany," he said. "You have nothing to worry about, Annie. You won't be outdone."

"I saw lemon sponge among the desserts," said Martin.

Arthur looked toward that table, where Madge Parsons and Martha Ward were in hot consultation.

"This does beat all," Martha was saying. "I *know* I sent two pumpkin and three mince." Martha gained at least ten pounds with every baby, Arthur thought, and though they had started nearly even when he'd first met her seven years ago, she now outweighed him by a good fifty. Another reason he preferred Emma Howe.

"You go on now," Arthur said to the Vogels. "I think I'll just step outside for a breath of fresh air."

He walked out into the night, leaving behind the stuffy room filled with talk and the clatter of plates and cutlery. He'd had enough party.

The sky had cleared—a rarity at this time of year—and the stars were out, thick clusters of them. No moon yet, but the whitened top of Mt. Pilchuck floated like an island in the sky to the east. The strong coffee of the supper had his pulse racing. A few people drifted out into the yard, children, mostly, tired of sitting still. A good night for walking, he thought. He'd just slip on out and head for home. No Elva. He couldn't believe his luck.

He walked back to the antechamber to collect his lantern and hat, pried open the stuck door, and stepped inside the murky room. The lamp still burned on the table, but someone had put a bucket over it, making a smell of hot metal and leaving only a crack of light. Before he could remove the bucket, two hands closed over his eyes.

"Hey, hey!" he said, startled. "It's dark enough in here already."

"Guess who?"

She'd been lying in wait for him. She had a voice like thick honey.

"Why, Mrs. Patrick Campbell," he said. "How nice of you to put North Falls on your tour. Forgive me for intruding into your dressing room."

She giggled and her voice got even huskier. "Guess again."

93

"Madge Parsons. Is that you? For shame."

The giggles got louder. "Guess again."

"I don't know. I'll have to give up."

"It's me, Arthur." She removed her hands from his eyes. "Couldn't you tell?"

"Why, it's Elva." He took the bucket off the lamp and lighted his lantern. It wasn't safe being in the dark with her, he thought. He reached for his hat.

"Don't go," she said. "You haven't said hello to me all night, though I waved to you three times up on the stage. You wouldn't even look my way. That's not friendly, Arthur Smollett, and you said neighbors must be friendly."

"I did say that," he agreed, "and you mustn't misconstrue my meaning. I meant friendship between myself and all the Browns, nothing more."

"Look," she said, "you're bleeding!" She plucked a handkerchief from her bosom, spat on it and dabbed at his temple. Her rubbing started his catbriar scratch to itching. She licked her finger and held it on the spot.

"Don't move," she said, "it'll soon stop. What would you do without me to look after you?" She stepped closer to him.

He could see the freckles across her nose, the fine white down that grew along the sides of her face below her ears. He felt the blood beat up in his throat and he wanted to kiss her. He tried hard to remember that she was his neighbor's daughter and wrote her N's backwards. Mostly, he concentrated on the rumors he'd heard about her with the Olsen boy last year. Such a woman was not for him.

"I have to tell you something, Elva," he said.

She had her mouth all pursed for what she must have sensed he wanted to do. "Yes?"

He set his lantern down, and his hat, the better to fend her off. She seized his hand and began to play with it.

"Remember when we read palms at Christmas? My step-mother said you had a short life line, but the longest heart line she'd ever seen. And a heart line stands for love."

He pulled his hand away. She couldn't have heard his news, or she wouldn't be throwing herself at him so hard, he thought.

94

"I have to tell you. I'm an engaged man now, or just about. I have a special friend coming by the train, Miss Emma Howe."

He felt guilty telling her. He had to admit that he'd flirted with Elva and imagined more than once bedding down with what made those polka dots so curvy. Denying it all the time, he'd led her on.

"Engaged," she said.

"Yes."

"Oh, you villain!" Her face went scarlet. Her cornflower eyes filled with angry tears, she slapped his face, and then bolted for the door in a swish of skirts. Swollen like all the others, the door stuck shut. She tugged, panting, then kicked it, then banged it with her fist. He stepped to help her, but she flashed him such a venomous look of "I'll get you for this" that he stopped in his tracks. She yanked violently, loosening one of her braids, and flew out of the room.

She'll cry rape, he thought, and I'll be ridden out of town on a rail.

He stood for a moment, trying to collect himself, then picked up his hat and lantern and went out into the yard. He'd danced with her at the Grange harvest fair once or twice, he thought, quickly reviewing his defense—but always in public view. He had never been alone with her until tonight. Those suppers at the Browns—a mistake, though who would have thought it. She'd seemed like one of the children trying out her feminine charms. He found her silly, but her wet finger on his temple had caused an unsettling stir in his groin.

He lingered in the side yard, bracing himself, then walked to the front of the hall where people were pouring out on their way back home. Best to be seen and put a bold face on it, he decided. Hal towered over an animated group. Arthur saw Annie and Martin setting off with their lantern down the road, no longer hand in hand the way they used to be. Over by the pump, Bert was getting a drink of water while his family loaded themselves into their wagon. He took the store teeth out, gave them a rinse, and put them in his breast pocket.

"Mr. Secretary," Bert hailed him, and came over to shake Arthur's hand with his—still wet from the pump though he wiped it on his trouser seat first. "I'll know where to come to have a letter written."

Bert's smile was back to normal, fangs guarding a cave with more than a little menace. Arthur was sure Bert was just buttering him up before he pounced.

"At your service," he said bravely. I never touched her, he said mentally, no matter what she's told you.

Bert leaned forward to speak confidentially. Here it comes, Arthur thought.

"Soon as I got home the other day, I told all the family your good news. They're in a stir to meet your visitor."

So Elva had known about Emma's coming and had come straight at him anyway with her seductive tricks. She was more scheming than he'd thought—no doubt the rumors about the Olsen boy were true. Arthur saw her out of the corner of his eye swinging her polka dots into the crowded wagon. She wouldn't look at him, which was just as well.

"Good night, Missus," he called to Bert's wife, Dee. "Good night to you all."

The children waved and called good night. As the wagon pulled out of the yard, drawn by Bert's patient team, eager now to get back to their barn, Elva gave Arthur an evil stare and then tossed her braids, stuck her chin up in the air, and looked away.

"Good night, Bert," Arthur called finally, and Bert gave a wave.

Thank goodness she'd not invented anything. He was apparently off the hook and he drew a long breath to celebrate. He hoped by the time he had walked home, he'd have his lust settled down and not have to resort to shameful bachelor tricks to go to sleep. Thank goodness, too, that Emma, so plain he knew she'd be his alone, was on her way. He needed a sanctioned place to take these feelings—inside a steady marriage to a good woman. He couldn't go on being at the mercy of bad little girls like Elva Brown.

XIII

WHEN EMMA disembarked at last, into evergreen forest, wood smoke, and rain, the one-room North Falls station was closed. She'd had to change trains one more time in Everett and was worn out with lugging baggage and hurrying to make the tight connection. That last scurry had slathered an icing of tiredness on her six-layered cake of fatigue. As she scanned the North Falls platform and found nobody, her right eyelid twitched and jumped. She was exhausted to the point of not really being able to see.

"My trunk?" she asked the conductor.

He jerked his thumb backward over his shoulder. "Baggage'll be up tomorrow. Passengers only on Sunday."

She had been, in fact, the only passenger.

The engineer descended from his lofty position, followed by the fireman, and the two of them, with the conductor, disappeared on the other side of the train, leaving her alone under the scanty station overhang with her luggage piled next to her unsteady knees. She'd wired Arthur from Spokane as to the exact time of her arrival, 8:06 P.M. on Sunday. She was sure of it and even had a copy of the wire in her purse. She peered into the drizzle toward the nearest building, Snows' Store according to its sign, which featured a long narrow porch, unpainted clapboards, a row of veiled second story windows, a steep shingle roof, and a smoking chimney. It had a barn and shed out back. Behind these buildings, fir trees closely packed as broom straws formed a shaggy backdrop that rose up and then disappeared in mist. It made the whole place seem not quite real, and her eyelid trembled as she tried to make her eyes focus clearly.

Then, at last, staring down the muddy road in front of the store, she spied a man on foot walking slowly toward the station. She made out his shape, his motion, his hat. She took a step forward, leaving the protection of the overhang, raising her hand, ready to call out in relief. It wasn't Arthur Smollett she saw. It was her father.

"Pa!" she called. He must have forgiven her for everything and come to save her! His face was beautiful—the aquiline nose, the bony jowls, the bright, deep sunk eyes. She'd done her best for him all her life, tried to be more than a perfect daughter, tried indeed to be his firstborn son. A gust of wind blew rain into her face and the apparition disappeared.

The pain of realizing it wasn't really Pa, plus the rain in her face, made her face her situation: nobody was there to meet her. Arthur—Mr. Smollett sounded better—had been unavoidably detained, or was carelessly late, or—had stood her up. I hope he dies, she thought. I hope a tree falls on him.

Fired by the heat of anger, she paced a moment, leaned against the wall, finally concluded: I need a place to sleep. She gathered up her possessions and made her way as best she could toward the light at the store.

Not a churchgoer, Arthur spent his Sunday mornings sleeping late and eating a large, leisurely breakfast. He caught up on the papers. He strolled about his ranch, assessing the stock and gardens, making plans. Having the rich earth under his feet and a bit of sun on his back—and no hoe or trowel in his hand—was a kind of worship for him.

Sunday afternoons were his time to visit or entertain guests. If nobody came to call, he did his accounts and wrote in his journal: weather, planting, harvesting. He noted community births and deaths, sales and purchases of property, unusual birds and animals. He liked to include comments on what he called "the human scene" and opinions of books he was reading. He recorded dreams if they struck him as interesting and reported on his "inner weather."

This Sunday he wrote:

The wet winter continues.

Annie Vogel feeling better after morning sickness. Martin looks pale and talks much of money. One of Hal's nephews, young Haskell, stepped on a nail but no lockjaw yet.

Have some business in Snohomish today. Emma Howe expected, 8:06 P.M. I am curious as a cat to meet her in person, but somewhat jumpy, too. Hope things are soon settled between us.

I have a heap of laundry.

He paused, unable or unwilling to set down in the journal what he hoped for in Emma. A hard, careful worker, of course. Not a complainer. A woman who could be happy, and her letters had seemed to promise that, for simple things amused her and gave her pleasure despite the limitations of her life. A friend who'd respond to his proposals with, "My, what good ideas you have!" Most of all—and here he remembered going to a dance with Hal when he was new in the county and how he'd felt when the caller sang out, "Ladies Choice!"—he wanted a beautiful stranger who would ask him to dance, hold him with her skirts and petticoats flying, whirl him right into the center of life.

Ordinarily he cleaned up in the evening to remove the day's grime, but this day he bathed after dinner, excited by the break in his normal routine, thinking of how he would appear to Emma, wanting to be at his best. He nicked a mole on his chin while shaving and tugged on a bootlace so hard it snapped in his hand. Not having a spare, he had to knot the frayed ends and then painstakingly rethread the lace from the knot outward in two directions so as to have even ends and enough to tie. He finished dressing feeling a bit frayed himself and not liking to have anything cobbled about his appearance. "For want of a bootlace, the lady was lost," he paraphrased to himself. He hoped Emma wouldn't hold a knot against him.

At midafternoon, he set out on Gray for the settlement of Snohomish, to contract with a small lumbering outfit to provide vegetables and fruit come June. He'd had the appointment to see the manager before Emma's wire had come, and it was not easy to change such things. He planned to transact his business with dispatch and then ride straight to the station.

He thought he had the directions to the manager's house

99

straight in his head, but somehow he missed a turning, went a quarter of a mile out of his way, had to backtrack, and wound up at the right place at last, but late.

"You mistook the fork for the main road," said the manager, Mr. Dodd, in a voice as colorless as water and as flat as slate. He was an iron-eyed man of forty with his sleeves rolled up over biceps as big as softballs. "Well, now that you're finally here, come in."

Mr. Dodd led Arthur into his hot little office, where Arthur, glancing at the clock over the cluttered rolltop desk, felt his stomach tighten. He hadn't thought he was that much behind. Well, signing the contract wouldn't take long and he'd push Gray to the limit on the way home. Forget about supper—there wasn't time. He could just make it, and if he were a little late back to North Falls, it wouldn't be by much.

"I'd like to go over your prices item by item," Mr. Dodd said, and Arthur's heart sank. But he hadn't come all this way to queer the deal. When the haggling was finally over and the deal struck, Arthur looked at the clock again and vaulted down Mr. Dodd's steps to Gray. He was really going to have to hump himself now.

He hoped he wouldn't be late—he didn't want to disappoint Emma after her long cross-nation odyssey. He didn't want to start off with her on the wrong foot. But he had to admit that he liked the image of pounding up to the station in a lather, arriving in the nick of time. He imagined himself and Gray pitted against the speed of the locomotive racing along its rails, and he felt wonderfully excited, like young Lochinvar coming out of the West, "Through all the wide Border his steed was the best." He whacked his hat against Gray's side and let out a whoop to get her started. Never mind what Mr. Dodd might think.

"He should be here to meet you," said Mrs. Snow behind the counter, but she smiled all the while as though nothing were seriously amiss. The rain suddenly drummed harder on the tin porch roof and Emma was glad to be indoors.

"Is there a place where I can rent a room?" she asked. The floor didn't seem entirely steady. The room smelled of pickles, tar, and cheese, good smells after the coal smoke of the train.

100

The fact that she'd at least arrived in the right place, and the welcome warmth from the stove, were making her want to cry, but she didn't want to cry in front of Mrs. Snow.

"We let rooms, since there's no hotel. I can give you the big one in front." Mrs. Snow took a lamp and Emma's valise and led her up the narrow stairs. "I expect you'd like a bath and something to eat."

Concealed in the shadows behind Mrs. Snow's full skirts, Emma cleared her brimming eyes with one finger. "Thank you," she said.

The room was chilly and sparsely furnished but clean—shiny floor, bright rag rug, tidy washstand, sparkling dresser, white, white bed. Mrs. Snow set the lamp in a hinged holder and lighted a candle.

"I'll heat some water, and there's soup left from supper. I'll call you when it's ready."

Forgetting her teeth, holding fiercely to her pride, Emma smiled her appreciation and Mrs. Snow smiled back—we know what men can be. Yes, but please don't say anything kind, Emma thought. The tears she wiped away could come flooding back at a moment's notice.

When Mrs. Snow bustled away, Emma's need to cry disappeared with her, partly because it was just too much effort. It was all she could do to tug off her shoes. Her feet expanded like dry sponges hitting water. She pulled off her smelly dress and petticoat. Her middle, the skin marked with a red line by tight waistbands, expanded like her feet. She put on her flannel nightdress and used the chamber pot, grateful for its immobility. She sat on the edge of the bed to take down her hair with arms almost too heavy to lift. When Mrs. Snow came to tell her that the soup was hot, Emma had fallen back across the white bedspread, dead asleep among the hairpins.

At 8:35 P.M., Arthur tied Gray in front of Snows'. Both of them were sweaty, tired, and hungry.

"Why, Arthur Smollett, for pity's sake, where on earth have you been?" said Millie Snow the moment he set foot inside. Her tone told him that, to her, he looked ridiculous, not valiant, and that he was in the doghouse for being late. He squelched an impulse to cut and run, scanned the room for an unfamiliar figure, saw none. He decided with Millie, at least, to put as bold a face on the situation as possible. He wasn't going to play the bad little boy to her scolding mother.

"I've been meeting the train," he told her, "but my passenger wasn't there."

Millie pointed at the clock. "Train was on time and so was Miss Howe. All that way to come and nobody to meet her. I wouldn't blame her if she never spoke to you again. You ought to be ashamed."

Millie had her arms folded and looked like a small, impregnable fortress. It was amazing, he thought, how women, even virtual strangers, took each other's parts.

"Business," he said briskly. "Couldn't be helped, and I got here as quick as I could. Well, where've you hidden her, Millie? Or did she turn around and go on back?"

Millie put her hands on her hips. "I wouldn't blame her if she did."

"Where is she now, then?"

"Upstairs. When I called her to take some soup, she'd fallen asleep on top of the covers, sideways across the bed. I had to tuck her in."

He turned his hat brim in his hand. Millie, he could see, was enjoying his discomfort. Probably hadn't had this much fun in days.

"So, you're too late, altogether." And serves you right, her expression added.

"Millie!" Harry poked his head in from the back hall. "Calf's coming. Come and lend a hand."

Millie gave Arthur a hard look and hurried out behind Harry, elbows cocked and hands raised in front of her in a show of self-important readiness. I've never been late for anything in my life, those hands said to him, and I'm not about to start now.

Left alone in the store, Arthur set his hat on the counter, put it on his head, took it off again, then slapped it once against his thigh. This wasn't how he'd planned things. Emma was supposed to have been a trifle worried, just this side of tremulous, and he was to have been the gallant rescuer. Now it turned out she had made an ally of the first North Falls resident she'd met

102

and popped off to sleep without giving him a second thought. He felt as though a war had begun and through losing the first skirmish, he'd lost the high ground. He felt terribly let down.

He was about to take himself home in defeat when he remembered writing his proposal in this very room. That night, too, Jip had been pasted to the floor by the stove as he was now and the Snows had been out back on important business. He remembered the buggy and the glory of his imagined ride in it with Emma. He couldn't just leave. They knew each other through letters. He'd come to feel close to her in letters. Letters were clear and safe, unlike real life. He'd at least leave her a note.

He found paper and an envelope behind the counter and wrote: *Dear Emma, I'm very sorry I wasn't at the station to meet you. I came as fast as I could, but was detained by business. I'll come by Monday after dinner. Perhaps we can take an afternoon walk. Your friend, Arthur.*

He sealed the envelope, put her name on the front, and left it on the counter for Millie to deliver. Getting back on Gray for the trip home, he felt he'd salvaged as much as he could of the situation. That was a good idea about going walking—they were both walkers, he knew from their exchanges in their letters—and he had often imagined his first stroll with Emma, when he'd get to really know her at last. It might even be better to see her for the first time tomorrow, when she'd rested up from her trip and he wasn't in such a state of mud and hunger himself. Now he had to get home with his tired horse. His hat was soaked, but he crammed it on his head and stepped out into the rain.

103

XIV

AFTER SLEEP and bathing—it was bliss to wash her hair —Emma dressed in the outfit she'd saved for meeting Arthur: cream shirtwaist, plum-colored six-gored skirt, deep purple cable-knit cardigan with bone buttons. She felt like herself in these clothes and knew they were "right" at home. She hoped to goodness they'd be "right" here. Then she went down to help Millie with the dinner.

Being careful to do only what Millie wanted done, she peeled potatoes and chopped onions, just like at home. She made a mistake when she asked for a cutting board—Millie sliced her vegetables right on the wooden counter. But she made up for any possible Eastern snobbery about cutting boards when she did the table wrong and Millie got to set her straight. Anyone should know, Millie's manner implied, that the forks didn't go on the left and the knives and spoons on the right. The knives and forks should be laid together at the tops of the plates and the spoons were taken, as needed, from a jar where they stood in the center of the table, bowls up.

When the Snow children came in for dinner and had washed, Harry commanded them to "Come and shake hands with Miss Howe."

Harry Junior—Sonny—did as he was told and promptly. He looked like a miniature of his father, right down to the blue wash shirt strained over a little pot belly. He was eight, maybe. John—Buddy—probably six, was pert like his mother and had to be urged to come and make his manners.

"Hello, Sonny, hello, Buddy," Emma said, shaking each cool

little pancake hand in turn. She refrained from asking, or worse, guessing, their ages, remembering how all her life people had guessed her young because she was small. She knew how that felt—to be thought six when you were eight, or twelve when you were fifteen. Often the guesser insisted on engaging you in a mocking battle to convince you that his low number couldn't be wrong, as though it defied belief that you really were the age you said you were. She had hated it—it had made her feel that the real Emma couldn't be seen. It seemed to her that in a lifetime of this kind of invisibility, Lydia—she recalled the moment on the train with fresh clarity—had been the only person to see her as she really was.

After dinner, nobody jumped up as they would have at home, to clear away the dirty dishes and hurry on with the next part of the day. Instead, Harry had more pie, Millie made another pot of coffee, and the little boys played at jackstraws in an alcove by the pantry door. Jip wandered in to see if there might be any tasty scraps and then wandered out again. Emma wondered if they were all hanging about to see her and Arthur meet, but it seemed so normal that she thought this might be the regular pace of life. She could hear Ma urging her, Anne and Maggie to gulp their last bites, "So I can get *done.*"

The Snows all looked very calm, but Emma was nervous and getting more so as the minutes went by. Her stomach rumbled, and Millie, hearing it, gave her a knowing look, whereupon Emma clattered a spoon to the floor. While she fumbled for it underneath the tablecloth, she heard footsteps and saw a strange pair of boots walk into the room, high, narrow leather boots with mud on the edges of the soles. One of the laces had a knot in it. She sat up hastily, without the spoon, her face flushed and her hair wisping where it had caught on the cloth.

It had to be Arthur because of his photograph, but he was shorter than she thought. Much shorter. And he had straight blond hair! He never said he was blond, and she couldn't tell from the sepia picture. She thought of Paul Goddard's dark hair, rich with waves and curls, and was painfully disappointed. She'd never been attracted to blond men, she realized all at once. He had a scabbed-over cut on his chin. He was wearing clothes like the ones in the photo—nothing special to mark the

105

occasion—and Ma's words rang in her ears: "At least he could have dressed himself up to have his picture taken." He seemed pleased to see her, but guarded, as though he didn't want his face to show too much of what he felt. As they exchanged glances, and his mouth smiled a greeting, his eyes, for a moment, revealed the look of a wary animal. Oh, dear, what had she gone and done? Alienated her family, come all this way, set herself up in this horribly awkward position. She didn't like him.

Arthur tried his best to conceal his nervousness. When he had first left home, he'd found that the way to survive on a sailing ship, close-packed with a lot of other boys and men, was to "play cowboy." The idea was to assume a tough, jaunty posture with your legs and shoulders, keep your face severely neutral, and speak as little as possible. If speech was necessary, you adopted a gruff tone, used irony, and "got" the other fellow in his weak spot before he "got" you.

After Arthur grew up a bit and especially after he came West to acquire his own place, he'd been able to discard most of this protective pose—though he still carried his legs and shoulders the way the first mate had, turned out to look "easy" and occupy the maximum amount of space. But meeting Emma, much as he'd longed for the moment, was slightly terrifying. When he looked at her across the Snows' dinner table and thought that she might soon march into his cabin and take over his life, he found himself reverting to the old protective style.

She didn't seem as young and sweet as she'd sounded in her letters. She had circles under her eyes. She was dressed as prissy as a schoolmarm. Her face didn't glow with adoration the way her letters had—*"You seem, in all you set your hand to, to show a true, manly, and independent spirit."* She seemed as she looked at him—and it hurt him badly to see it—disappointed. So he played cowboy in his own defense. He had a gift for her in his jacket pocket, but at the moment, he forgot it was there. Certainly he forgot the tenderness that had made him want to give her a present.

"Afternoon, folks," he said, twirling his hat twice around on his finger. He greeted Emma as though he'd known her all his life. "Afternoon, Emma. Glad to see you finally made it."

106

His words came out more brusquely than he'd meant them to, but he wasn't able to fine tune his voice. He felt as though everything, including himself, was a little out of control. He glanced from her face to her breasts, small but nicely shaped beneath her cable-knit sweater. Attracted, he smiled at her again, but she was rattled by his first words and did not see his admiration. She felt he was laughing at her bone buttons, and she felt herself fussily overdressed.

His tone was not what Emma expected—she wasn't happy to be accused of lateness, *his* fault. No welcome to Washington, no inquiry about her trip, no handshake or verbal apology for not meeting her train. Not only blond, but rude, she thought—not like in his letters. In his very first letter, the one in response to her poem, he'd said the bloodroot blossoms were "as big as teacups." He had described the ferns poking up through the earth "like curled fingers." She had felt he was a kindred spirit, someone who saw the world as she did, but now he seemed bent on holding her off. Perhaps he'd seen the disappointment on her face, though she'd tried quickly to conceal it. Maybe this was just rough Western manners. Now, she felt the Snows watching to see how she would take his remark. She was anguished to think she'd made a terrible mistake, fallen in love with a man who didn't exist and pursued him for three thousand miles only to find this—stranger. But she had her Yankee pride, and if she felt anguished, she would never let it show.

"*You're* too late for dinner, Mr. Smollett," she said with as much spirit as she could muster. "Though I expect Millie will give you coffee, since she's a friend of yours."

"If you can spare the time," said Millie, dryly, apparently glad to play along. "Sonny, fetch Mr. Smollett a chair."

Arthur refused coffee but sat, across the table from Emma. Careful not to stare, she observed his face, trying to find features to approve and to match the idealized picture she'd carried in her mind since last spring. He had a long nose, bright eyes, stubborn chin. His ears were close to his head, not fleshy and flabby like Roland's. He was freshly shaved and had awfully clean nails for a farmer—maybe he had made an effort on her behalf after all.

107

He observed her observing him. "How was your trip?" he asked at last.

"I seem to be in one piece." She noticed for the first time since her arrival how her Vermont accent stood out among these Westerners. She felt herself a foreigner.

"You pronounce like my people," he said. "I expect I've lost a good bit of it by now."

"You sound all right," Harry said. "Hal says you talked funny when you came."

"I can hear traces," Emma said. That, at least, was pleasant about him.

Millie, who had been hovering by the stove, couldn't contain herself any longer. "Is she what you thought?" she demanded of Arthur.

He looked at Emma steadily. Her teeth weren't as bad as in her picture, or maybe she just didn't seem as worried about them, and her eyes were better, dark and luminous. A man could fall in love with those eyes. He wished he hadn't seen that flash of disappointment in them. What was she expecting him to be—Rob Roy or Mr. Lincoln?

"Pretty much," he said.

"And what about you, Miss Howe?"

Emma returned his gaze as best she could, but everything she saw made her feel worse. To go with his blond hair, he had blue eyes, which she had never liked, either. She did like his smile, but he was so—short. Oh, what *had* she done—invented someone, fallen in love with her invention, and sacrificed her entire former life for this stranger with a knot in his bootlace?

"Time will tell. I *did* expect to be met at the station."

"Now you're in trouble, Arthur," Harry said.

"Good for you, Miss Howe," said Millie.

"If you folks will excuse us," said Arthur, "I think I'll just show Miss Howe around a bit."

He felt a lot better on the front porch without the Snows looking on. Looking at the endless banks of shaggy evergreens and the unfamiliar sky, Emma felt her brave show of indignation collapse like a tent whose pegs are pulled. She had no real support here. She felt stupid to have risked alienating the one person who was meant to be her friend. But he was so different

108

from what she'd thought. It was none of it the way it was supposed to be.

"Does it rain a lot here?" she asked, just to be saying something, and was appalled to hear her voice squeak out of her throat, thin as a girl's.

"In winter it does."

"Our winters back East are all snow and cold," she said, forgetting in her discomfort that he was from Somerville and knew all about Eastern weather. "Never any rain and everything in white, not gray. We had three feet on the ground the day I left, and more coming. I smelled snow in the air on the way to the station. Our hired man drove me. You can smell snow, you know—it's a sort of dusty smell with a lot of dampness to it, like the air before a rain but colder, of course. That's a time I love, right before a rain, and when the first drops hit the dust, I love that smell. I don't suppose you ever get that smell out here. Does it rain here all the time?" When the question was out, she heard his long silence, a palpable pause. She realized to her embarrassment that she'd been chattering and that she had already asked him about the rain.

"In winter. Only in winter."

"Oh. Thank goodness—only in winter."

"I wrote to you about the rain."

"I don't remember. I suppose you did."

"I guess you're still mad."

"Oh, no. Well, I suppose I am."

He laughed shortly. "Make up your mind."

"I *am* mad." It was one of the bravest moments of her life. "I came a long way."

"Well, I guess you have a right to be," he said. "I had to see a man about a contract, and one thing after another came up to make me late. Believe me, I tried as hard as ever I could to get to the station when the train came in."

He coughed. She was silent, hearing the sincerity in his voice, but feeling that he could never know what it had done to her to arrive, imagine she saw her father, and find that she had to make her own way in an unknown place, abandoned for whatever reason by the person she had counted on to be there. The aloneness of people—their essential unknowable quality—

109

struck her as it had on occasion in the past but never with such force. How could she and Arthur ever reach each other?

"When I set out from Mr. Dodd's," Arthur said, "I thought I might make it in the nick. And I suppose I thought to have an advantage, being a *little* late. But I was far later than I meant, and now I see I've lost it."

"I was nervous to meet you."

"I wasn't too easy about it myself. Nor am I what you'd call comfortable right now. But I haven't lost all of my Eastern manners. I apologize. I said that in my note and I meant it. It's not how I meant for things to begin for us. I hope you'll forgive me."

"I accept your apology," Emma said.

For a few moments, neither of them spoke. She knew she'd never forget that he didn't meet her train. But she was mollified by his apology, and impressed by his confessing that he'd thought to have a bit of advantage. Here, shoulder to shoulder with her on the porch, with no audience, and not forced to meet her gaze right across a table, he seemed more like the person in the letters even though his looks were wrong.

"I'd like to go walking, like you said in your note, if you still want to," she said. She thought of how she'd imagined them together looking for violets and bloodroot, but it was much too early for spring flowers. And that was just a fantasy of the letters. They had to start over, from scratch. From blondness.

"Cold day for a hike, but we could go see the Falls. There'll be mud."

"Vermonters know all about mud."

"Well, come along, then." A bit stiffly, he offered her his arm and a bit stiffly she took it. Gray, seeing Arthur coming, gave a hopeful nicker. "This is my horse," Arthur said.

"Oh," said Emma. "What a nice one." Gray looked sleek and well-tended. Arthur smoothed his hand down the side of Gray's neck. The horse nickered again.

"She's wanting to go home," Arthur said.

"Yes," said Emma, "home," and suddenly she felt the emotional ground slide out from under her feet. She wanted her cat, Tom, and her warm, familiar kitchen. She wanted her family in all their cantankerousness, as they had been before she'd ever

110

heard of Arthur Smollett. She wanted to be in Warwick, and she leaned her forehead against the horse's shoulder and started to cry.

"Whatever is the matter?" Arthur asked, aghast.

"Nothing," Emma said, hiding her face against Gray and pushing back her tears. "You have a beautiful horse."

Hastily she dried her eyes and took his arm again. They started down the wooden sidewalk, skirting the rotten places. His long strides and her short steps didn't match, and they bumped along, Arthur almost pulling her. He let go her arm. Crying about my horse, he thought. What on earth—?

They walked more easily when the sidewalk ended and they had room on the wider dirt road, but he was stumped if he could think of anything to say. What had she been crying about, for heaven's sake? She seemed healthy, he thought. Small and thin, but sappy. She was clever enough. He'd read about arranged marriages some place in the world. I suppose it don't matter if we like each other, so long as we can get along, he thought. He felt like a man who had ordered a large, expensive item from a catalogue and now might have to arrange for a return.

All Emma could think of was how her heart would leap when she saw her name in his handwriting, how she would run upstairs to her room to read his letter four or five times in private. She must have been bewitched, to be so in love with an imagined Arthur. She wished she liked him now.

XV

"THEY'RE NOT really falls!" Emma shouted over the noise of the water. To her "falls" meant Niagara, shown in dramatic pictures in a Sunday Supplement feature about a high-society honeymoon. A great wall of falling water, a cloud of rising spume. North Falls got its name from a wide stretch in the Stillaguamish River where it cascaded over big granite boulders. Impressive, but in Emma's book, not "falls."

"It ought to be North Cascades!" she shouted.

Arthur thought—how picky can you get. "Too hard to say," he shouted.

"What?"

"*Cascades* is too hard to say!" he shouted into her ear.

Emma shrugged. He couldn't tell if that were a concession to his point or to the river's roar. Conversation on the walk out had been strained at best. Now that they had something to talk about, they couldn't hear each other. But he hadn't been able to think of anywhere else to take her. The Falls was a popular picnic spot in summer. Today they were the only visitors. He looked around at the glistening granite outcropping backed by blue-green branches. Up above, the peaks to the east were shrouded in mist. He cast about for something else to amuse her.

"Mt. Rainier's down that way," he shouted. " 'Course you can't see it from here." He'd stopped at the lookout on the way to Everett more than once and been lucky enough to have a crystalline view of the snow-capped peak, which stood up sharp as a knife blade. It was nine thousand feet higher than those poor old Vermont foothills eroded by the glaciers, that Emma had put into her letters. He wished he could make Mt. Rainier appear right now, or Mt. Pilchuck—even it would fill the bill. The sun was out at the Falls—it was really quite a nice day, he thought—but Mt. Pilchuck was fogged in. He willed the clouds to part in revelation like the Red Sea, but the pale gray blankets over to the east, several miles thick, merely wisped, shredded, and rewove themselves.

"Mt. Rainier's quite a sight," he shouted, frustrated.

She shrugged again, as if to say—if you say so.

He had hoped the Falls would impress her, which would lead to his being more comfortable with her, which would lead to a quiet time of mutual admiration of nature—which was what had brought them together in the first place through her poem —which would lead to his being able to kiss her. But clearly she wasn't impressed. He felt as though he were trying to dance with a cigar-store Indian. And though the weather was cooperating with his plans, at least locally, there wasn't any place dry to sit.

"Might as well go back," he shouted, and she nodded with a bit more alacrity than he liked to see. Again, he cast about for ways to amuse her. They'd come to the Falls by the road over the bridge.

"I'll take you back on the trail through the woods," he said, as soon as they could hear themselves speak. Maybe they'd see an interesting bird or animal and that would do the trick, but after her reaction to an invisible mountain, he thought it best not to make any promises.

"Fine," she said.

They started down the road to where the trail cut off. He thought her week on the train might be good for a bit more talk. She'd lighted up when he'd asked her about it.

"You had an interesting trip out here, then."

"Oh, yes." She'd told him about seeing the Rockies and the plains, about Emily Dodge and Lydia. She tried to think of more to tell him, but all that volunteered itself was the story of the young couple—the girl who had the blackberry jam—and how she and her young man had made love in the seat behind her. She wasn't about to tell him that.

113

"Your family finally approved of your coming?"

"Not exactly. But I came, nevertheless."

"So, what do you think of North Falls so far?" He meant, what do you think of me.

"It seems all right." To her, speaking Vermont, "all right" meant "very good," but he heard it as "passable." He felt as if he was poking a dozen keys at a lock, but so far none had slid in.

"Have you written any new poems lately?"

Emma glanced at him in surprise. She'd been in a state of chaos for the past three weeks, deciding, packing, traveling, getting to a strange new place. How could she possibly have been writing poems? Besides, she'd come to think since she had left Vermont that "Bloodroot" was pretty thin stuff when you came right down to it. All she could remember was the first four lines: *Despairing, weary, much in need of grace, / I hunt and find you on the mountainside, / Snowy petals, green leaf edged with lace, / 'Tis then I know the deadly winter's died.* She remembered adoring those words when she'd written them, but she didn't much like them any more. "Despairing, weary" —the poem sounded whiny. She didn't like to think she'd felt that sorry for herself.

"No," she said. Strange, that the poem that had started them writing to each other she didn't much like any more.

He tried again. "It'll be bloodroot time soon. There's quite a bit of it on the ridge behind my place."

She heard him trying, and this time she felt a touch of admiration for his doggedness. She remembered how, on the store porch, he'd admitted he had planned to be just a little late "to have an advantage." That was honest—he hadn't had to tell her that. She didn't want to talk about bloodroot, but she'd heard his voice caress the words "my place," and saw a chance to move away from his contrived questions.

"Tell me about your ranch," she said.

He looked like a drowning man who had been thrown a rope, and he began to talk. His hands moved in expressive gestures, and his body lost its stiffness, as he mapped out the ridges, the creek he had created, and the general shape of the valley. When they turned onto the trail, and came to a slippery bank, he took her arm to help her and he no longer felt made of wood.

He let her arm go when they were safely down, needing both hands to describe the orchard, barn, cabin, gardens, and berry bushes. It was like listening to Pa talk about the Creamery, she thought, except that she was interested in the subject, not just in having Pa's attention. The admiration she felt for him when he wrote to her about homesteading came back, and she thought of the old riddle about the tree falling and no one hearing so perhaps there was no sound. If a man cleared a ranch alone in the wilderness and nobody appreciated it, did it really happen?

He was describing his plans to construct an underdrain.

"How do you keep it from clogging?" she asked.

"I don't quite have that part figured." He looked at her in surprise. He was used to dealing with these problems alone, but she'd really been listening and had asked a logical question.

"Got any ideas?" he asked.

"What about a heavy wire mesh over the pipe ends? Something between screening and turkey wire for size."

"That might work."

They were nearing the stream with its stepping stones, almost back to where the trail rejoined the road and led quickly into town. This part of the walk hadn't been so bad. He remembered that she had admitted she'd been afraid to meet him. Maybe she was just shy, just needed a little time—it was only natural.

"I expect you'll need something to keep the pipes clear," she said, "what with all the rain you get out here."

He looked up at the clear sky and the sun filtering down on the trail. "Rain?"

"Yes—it's done nothing but since I arrived."

"You call this rain? Sky looks pretty good to me."

All she could think of was standing alone on the train platform because he hadn't shown up. And the cold gust of water she'd gotten in the face when she stepped off to meet the figure she'd thought was Pa.

"I admit it's not raining this very second. But it seems like that's all it does. Millie told me. And you said yourself."

"In winter. I said in winter."

"This *is* winter."

"We're coming up on February, our driest month till spring. You've come at a good time. This is a beautiful day."

She shook her head, no. "North Falls is a wet place."

"I never said it wasn't. But spring is pretty good and the summers are wonderful—as dry and warm as you please. You can see a view of Mt. Pilchuck all summer long."

"No view till summer?" She looked as though he'd said they wouldn't eat till the Fourth of July.

He drew a breath, trying to be patient. "We're coming to the stream," he said. "The one we crossed on that bridge when we were on the road. There's stepping stones here, or should be." If the winter rain hasn't moved them, he added to himself.

But she was not to be distracted. "No view till summer? And no sun till then? I should think you'd all be dead of gloom and mildew."

"Listen," he said, "I didn't much like the rainy weather either, when I first came. But you get used to it and the winter's not forever. The ladies say it's good for their complexions. Makes their hair curl."

They stood by the stream bed and he saw that, indeed, the stepping stones had been dislodged. Some had moved, some were underwater, and some were gone altogether. He looked anxiously at Emma's skirt and shoes.

"What ladies?" she asked.

"My neighbors. Annie Vogel, who's having a baby soon, and Martha Ward, my best friend's sister." And to himself he added —and Elva Brown, who'd actually said it, calling attention to her own complexion of peaches and cream that the weather couldn't improve upon. He felt himself color up a bit, and he noticed that Emma noticed.

"All I know about the rain," she said briskly, "is that it poured the night I came, it rained all this morning so my washing couldn't dry, and any fool can see it's going to rain again any minute. It's practically all you wrote about, the wet weather. And now how do you propose I get across this river you've brought me to?"

That tone got him. It was Somerville—she even said "rivah" —and Mrs. Melvin Smollett, alias his mother, handing out the blame. In an angry rush, he picked up a few of the largest rocks

116

near by and heaved them into the spaces in the stream. *Stream* —not "rivah." It was a pleasure to hear them splash noisily and see her jump back to keep herself dry. They were pretty far apart, but she'd jumped back nimbly enough. Let her do a bit more jumping.

"There," he said. "Now, follow me."

He moved decisively toward the water's edge, happy to be taking charge at last after a morning of fruitless efforts to woo her, confident that she'd be right behind. But when he glanced over his shoulder, to make sure she was there, she gave him such a look of resistance as he'd never had before from anything smaller than a redwood. He watched astonished as she found a rock of her own to perch on, took off her shoes, peeled off her stockings, and holding the shoes in one hand and the stockings in the other, waded into the stream. Waded right into the center. And waded out on the other side. He hurried across his stepping stones as fast as dignity permitted, being careful on a couple that were unsteady—he wasn't going to fall in, not if he could help it. By the time he reached her, she was seated on another rock, smiling quite a bit and drying her feet on her petticoat. At least they were bright red—that stream, he happened to know, as she didn't, was pure melted snow at this time of year.

"Looks like you've got some pretty cold feet there," he said.

She hadn't really smiled at him yet, and he'd figured it was because of her teeth, but she looked up now and the smile he saw was brilliant, radiating out of her eyes and her mouth and her whole face at once. The trouble was it wasn't for him.

"Is that so?" she said, meaning—you can go fry ice, forever. "For your information, my feet have never felt better."

By the time they got back to the store, he knew it was over, even before she made her little speech about being sorry, and wishing that it might have worked out between them. When he remembered her "Is that so?" he wasn't even disappointed, just glad to be shut of her, though he knew he was in for a lot of nosy questions and a hard time from people—everyone—who knew he'd invited her to come. And there was her future, too—he couldn't as a man of honor not concern himself with her plans. After all, he'd sent her the money for her ticket.

"I suppose you'll be going back to Warwick," he said. They were talking well out of earshot of the store, both, he realized, wanting to avoid any more embarrassment if they could. "I can help you out with that, of course."

Her face softened, and he knew she was touched. "I wouldn't hear of it," she said. "And I'm not going back."

"You're not?"

"I didn't tell you the whole of it," she said. "I had an awful fight with my pa before I left. I can't go back there, nor do I want to."

He felt responsible for her, even if he couldn't manage her and even if, as was clearly true, she didn't like him much. He'd never once on the whole walk felt her body saying "kiss me," as he felt it every second from Elva Brown. He wouldn't have minded trying—there was something about those large dark eyes—but he wasn't going to put his foot in a bear trap. But he rather liked the idea that she couldn't or wouldn't return to Vermont.

The look he gave her said—well, then, you're marooned. Maybe you'd better stick it out with me.

She really didn't know what she would do, until that second. She hadn't given it any thought. But now, challenged by that look, by his assumption that he was her only option, she made something up, out of whole cloth, as Ma used to say, created a brand new quilt without a pattern. She'd spent the morning with Millie in the kitchen, drying her hair and doing her laundry. She hadn't realized she'd been collecting pieces, but now, quick as a finger snap, she started putting them together.

"I hear Seattle's a boomtown these days," she said. "Lots of prospectors getting outfitted, and new people moving into town. I'm a seamstress, you remember, and I had my own shop for a time. Millie's got a sister in Seattle with some children that she needs help minding. I'll go there and get work, maybe run my own shop again quite soon."

He couldn't believe his ears—he thought he'd had her cornered when she said she wasn't going home—but here she'd come up with some hairbrained scheme, to go to Seattle, of all places, where there was nothing but noise, scheming, and riffraff. Oh, she had misled him badly, with her quiet, poetic letters

118

about wild flowers. He was about to tell her to go, and good riddance, when he saw in those eyes of hers that she was only two-thirds defiant. The other third was scared—but she was going to do it anyway. He knew what that amounted to. If you were scared, and knew it, and showed it, but went ahead and did it, whatever it was, anyway—you were brave.

"Well, I guess you'd better give Seattle a try, then," he said.

"Yes," she said. "I will."

XVI

OVER THE next few days, Emma prepared to move to Seattle. She talked further with Millie and wrote to Millie's sister. It turned out she was needed, but the sister wanted some time to clear the spare room. Emma wrote to an outfitter Harry knew, and also wrote to some of Millie's sister's friends about doing family sewing.

In the meantime, she helped out with the store and minded Sonny and Buddy after school in exchange for her room and board. Evenings she sat with the Snows in their big kitchen, working on her quilt and listening to talk of North Falls. She was glad for the chance to gather her strength before launching out again. She didn't see Arthur, and she tried not to think about Pa. Millie said Arthur came in now at four o'clock—must have learned that Emma'd be busy with the children then. In the whole beginning of February, it didn't rain once.

"Ain't this dry spell peculiar?" Martin Vogel asked Harry Snow when he came to the store to collect the mail.

"Ain't it?" Harry responded.

Two questions, Emma thought, that were really answers.

"Why does God send us no rain?" Amos Brill asked in Jeremiah tones. Everyone in his vicinity moved a step away.

"What do you make of this drought?" Madge Parsons asked Millie one day when she and Emma were behind the counter.

"Emma brought it," Millie said pertly, and Emma almost felt she had.

Arthur's neighbors were the customers. One day a woman whose face was etched all over with deep curving parallels

120

came in, sat by the stove, and nursed her baby, plugging a tough and long brown nipple into its mouth. The baby smacked and snuffled, noisy as a dog licking out a jar. Emma thought of her sister Anne, who always retreated with her twins to an upstairs bedroom for feedings and even there discreetly draped a shawl.

"When you've had as many as I have," the woman said, catching Emma's eye, "you won't think twice. You must be Emma. I'm Dee Brown."

"Glad to meet you," Emma said.

"Glad to sit here awhile," Dee said. "Anything to get out of the house."

After Dee had fed her baby and made her purchases, she went out to her wagon and sent a sulky blond girl to carry out the groceries. The girl lugged out one box and came back for the second. As she pulled it into her arms across the counter, she sized up Emma and lifted her chin. "I can beat you up," she said just before she left.

"Whoever was that?" Emma asked Harry, who'd been cutting up beef with his back turned during this encounter.

"That's Elva Brown, Bert's oldest, Dee's stepdaughter."

"A special friend of Arthur's, maybe?" Emma remembered how he'd colored up over the idea that the rain was good for ladies' complexions and made their hair curl.

Harry wiped the blood off his hands onto his apron and gave the matter a moment's thought. "Arthur might have wanted to snitch some plums, but he never would have gone for the whole cobbler."

One day when Emma was minding the store alone, an enormous bearded man arrived, smoothing a crumpled paper and trying to make it out.

"Can't seem to figure what Martha wants from this, B.P.'s what she wrote, do you think that might be biscuit pans? Couldn't be, she's got enough of those, berry pails? A box of prunes?"

"Baking powder, most likely," Emma suggested, having heard of Martha's large family and reputation as a cook.

"Of course! You're a wonder, you must be Emma, Arthur said you were clever and now you've saved the day not to mention another trip if I'd gone home with black pepper or brown

121

paper, she said this morning she was fresh out of baking powder."

"Then that must be it," Emma said while the giant wrung her small hand in his enormous one and she hoped he wouldn't say, "How's the air down there?"

"I'm Hal Landis and I just want you to know I think Arthur's making a big mistake in not keeping you here though Seattle's a wonderful place, you'll like it, I go down pretty often, maybe I can help you meet some folks and get settled, though Arthur's a chump to let you go, he never does go after things hard enough, only on the ranch, but not women or deer. He hangs back just when he should move forward, he's got to learn better timing if that's what it is, he's my best friend but he can be an awful dunce." Hal let go her hand and moved toward the door, fast for such a large person. Emma ran after him.

"Don't forget your baking powder." When he dropped it into his jacket pocket, she heard the tin cylinder clunk onto a bed of nails.

"Martha'll be inviting you to supper," he said. "Don't go until she does."

Bert Brown came one day with his two little girls and asked Emma to mind them while he and Harry took some barrels of fish down to the train.

After the Browns had left, Millie said, "My Buddy and Sonny don't play with the Brown girls much, though they're of an age. But they'll play with the Brown boys any day, even though they're older. In general, they're antigirl."

"They're nice girls," Emma said. "Molly read a page from her primer to me, and she's only six. Jane has four dolls, that she made herself out of sticks with the faces drawn on and dresses from her mother's scrap bag. A mother, father, son, and daughter, she said they sometimes were, or sometimes a mother and three babies. Today, though, they were four sisters who were orphans."

"Kids," Millie summed up, "they sure know how to get under your skin." Emma decided not to mention that she, Anne, and Maggie had played orphans by the hour.

By the middle of February, she'd made her arrangements and was ready to move on, though of course by then North Falls didn't seem so bad. But it was too small to support a full-time seamstress, and Arthur's presence was a continuing source of pain. What a fool she'd been, what a bundle of mistakes they'd made, from start to finish. She didn't want to see him again. She decided to write when she was settled in Seattle, at least thank him for being the reason she'd left home. No matter what, that part had been good.

She had her train ticket bought and was just finishing up her packing in the evening, set to travel the next day, when she smelled smoke. Not just a whiff from someone's chimney— everyone in town heated with wood. Too much smoke—too thick and too black and too near. She was starting to run down the stairs, when she heard Millie shouting up them.

"Come help me, Emma! The barn's on fire!"

The two women met in the hall and hurried out through the kitchen.

"I got the cow and calf," Millie said, "and tied them out front of the store. But we've got to get the horses."

"I'll get one and you take the other," Emma said. "Where's Harry?"

"Taking the mail down for the morning train—should be back any time. But we've got to get the animals safe first. The horses and then the chickens."

Emma thought—maybe it's not so bad yet—maybe we should stop the fire first and save the barn *and* the animals, but when she stepped outside, she saw Millie was right. The fire, which had started in a cow stall, had already leaped up and caught the hay. From the hay, it was just another leap to the roof. And from the stall, it had already moved across the waist-high divider into the adjoining shed. It was so fast, so eager for anything dry and loose, the blankets hanging on the shed wall, the pile of kindling stacked against that wall on the other side to keep it out of the wet. The fire was way past being quenched by a bucket or two of water, and if they didn't get the horses out right then, it would be too late. She put her arm over her nose to protect herself from smoke, dashed in through the wide doors, and threw a rope halter over the neck of Beauty, one of the frightened beasts.

"Ho, now," she said, trying to sound in charge. She backed

123

him out of the stall, turned him, and trotted him through the billowing smoke and into the yard. Around front, Millie had said, where she'd tied the cow and calf. The two women met again at the railing.

"I'm going to get the children," Millie said, "in case it spreads to the house. The wind's in that direction, and it would only take a spark—it's been so dry. See if you can get the chickens—just open the door and they'll run."

Emma couldn't believe that Millie, who sometimes got rattled when the store got full, or yelled at Sonny and Buddy just because she'd had enough noise and was tired, could be so calm.

"Shouldn't one of us go for help?" she asked.

"Not till everyone's safe—then you can run and ring the church bell."

The chicken coop was built against the far barn wall, so at least she didn't have to go inside again. That was a blessing, Emma realized as she ran by, because inside was now ablaze. She rounded the corner, relieved to get away from the flames, and yanked open the hen house door. The chickens ran in circles till she shooed them out. She checked the corners for birds too stupid to save their own lives. Once out, they seemed to know enough to scuttle away from the smoke and heat—too much like a Sunday oven, she thought, and was shocked to have time for such a thought when there seemed to be so much to do.

But in fact, there wasn't much more to do once the animals were rescued. She rounded the barn again and was pushed by the heat over next to the house. The barn was a goner, and the shed—oh, with Harry's wonderful buggy, which he was so proud of!—the shed and buggy were caught and blazing, too. She thought of what Millie had said about sparks, the dry spell, and the house, but felt powerless there alone. Ring the church bell, she remembered, and then heard it begin to toll—Millie, or Harry, or somebody was at least doing that. She moved carefully across the yard, her arm raised to protect her face against the smoke and heat, and then, thank God, there were suddenly other people to help. There was Millie returning from the church, and Harry with her, and there, coming down the road on Gray, was Arthur Smollett.

He walked into the yard, nodded to her, and said, "That back

124

kitchen roof could catch, and that would mean the house. We need a bucket brigade. Get the buckets from the store, Emma, that stack of brand new tin ones that just came in. Harry, get your ladder—I know you keep it leaning against the barn wall, far side of the chicken house. Always thought you should put it inside, but tonight I'm glad you don't. Lean it against the kitchen, this side, farthest from the fire, closest to the pump. Millie, you form the line from the pump to the ladder. Put the strongest ones at the end—to hand the full buckets up the hill. If we can wet down that roof, and the back kitchen wall—"

This was not the tone he'd used about the stepping stones, where he was going to show her who was boss. This was a clear, urgent plan needing everyone's help. Even as she ran for the buckets, Emma thought—he knows just where everything is and what's to be done—and she admired his good sense and self-possession. A man who could keep his wits about him in the face of a fire was—all right.

So they formed their little line against the bright, hot fire blazing up overhead, and Emma knew she'd never worked so hard in her life, not even at haying, which could break a person's back. People heard the bell and came. Hal pumped, Martin was in line on one side of Emma, and Millie was on her other side, but there were others, too, people she'd only started to know through the store—the folks who worked at the finishing mill, the station master who also taught the school, women who'd got their children out of bed and left them on the store porch to come and fight the fire. Jason Parsons, who reminded Emma of Pa, for he was made much the same right down to the nose and eyes, was at the top of the ladder and pitched the water across the roof. Amos Brill stood on the ladder below Parsons, and Madge, who wasn't much use in the line for she got too out of puff, minded the children. The buckets came up full and went back empty, and when the barn roof was about to cave in, they all ran for the road, even though they felt too soaked themselves with water and sweat to be in danger. But Parsons from his vantage point called out for them to run, so they did, and were glad they had when they saw how far the flaming debris flew. A couple of pieces hit the kitchen roof and sizzled out. Another hit and smouldered. The brigade reformed and Parsons aimed his shots as best he could till he squelched it. Then, with the barn down and the worst of the danger over, they watched for more sparks to fly but stopped their work.

Emma, soaked from foot to waist, heard Millie, standing beside her, stifle a sob and took her hand. She looked around for Arthur, then picked him out where he must have been in the line, next to Hal. The two men, one so large and the other small and sinewy, both smudged with ashes, weren't talking, just watching what was left of the fire. They looked more somber than victorious, for though the house had been saved, the barn and shed were gone.

Emma wanted to join them, to stand next to Arthur in the dark as a way of nullifying her breaking things off between them. She wanted to hear him say something that had a "we" in it, in which she was included. If he would look at her and say, "We did a good job of work tonight"—anything like that—she would be happy. But she knew she couldn't intrude on him and Hal. She needed an invitation. She let go Millie's hand, but still she hovered in the shadows, unable to approach him. Then through the darkness, she saw him smile at her. A flare from the dying fire caught one side of his face and two overlapping side teeth in his smile, giving it a warm friendly shine. She returned it, full force. She'd gotten her "we."

Harry, who Emma thought would be in a state of mourning over his buggy, went from person to person, thanking people. His pants and shirt had long since parted company in the effort of the night, but Emma thought he'd never looked more dignified. Then folks began to realize it was one in the morning and to straggle home, the stink of smoke and ashes in their clothes and hair.

Emma sponged off the worst of the filth so she wouldn't soil Millie's sheets. Her hands were swollen from handling the bails of heavy buckets. Her shoulders ached and the smell of smoke clung to her, seeming to have taken up residence right inside her nose. But she was glad that she'd been there to help, and she was even gladder about what she'd seen of Arthur and what had passed between them, about that little rekindled moment. After being in the bucket brigade and soaked with sweat and water, he hadn't looked so blond. He hadn't looked blond at all.

126

He'd looked dark and—manly, like the Arthur in her letters. Tired as she was, she wished fleetingly that Arthur were here in bed with her, just to hold her, just to touch.

All of the fire fighters were asleep an hour later when it began to rain.

XVII

THE DAY after the fire, Arthur was up at five for the morning chores. He'd told Martin to take the day off—no sense in them both running short on sleep. After milking, and feeding the chickens, he was too awake to go back to bed, so he had breakfast, wondering why his spirits were so low. It wasn't just the letdown after last night's excitement. He remembered that today was when Emma was leaving for Seattle—he'd heard that from any number of folks. He hadn't seen her till last night, and now he realized he didn't want to let her go without any kind of good-bye.

He'd been too whipped last night to clean up well, so he bathed, shaved, and looked in the mirror, wondering what any woman might ever see in him. His face was nothing special. He looked too serious and didn't smile enough. He trimmed his moustache, afraid that it was getting "droopy," that Emma would find him old and dull. He realized he'd been sentimental about her, wanting to take her for buggy rides and commune with her at waterfalls. But stripped of those romantic notions, he felt himself to be a drab rationalist. He grew rutabagas. He designed underdrains. He knew five different kinds of apple scab. If one of his gates wouldn't close tight, he'd work all day to get it to fit. How could any woman be attracted to such a person? Even Elva, for all her flirting, didn't love him. He was just practice to her, an old sock that a puppy pretends is a snake so he can learn how to break its neck with shaking.

He realized he was in no mood to go to town, but also that he was going anyway. He'd seen Emma when they were fighting

128

the fire, and he'd liked the idea—sentimental again—that the full bucket Hal passed to him had gone on down the line from his hands to hers before it went even farther to the roof. He knew there'd be a lot of folks around the store this morning, looking at the damage and recounting last night's events. It might be a little awkward, everyone knowing he'd invited her from Vermont and that she'd turned him down. But that couldn't be helped. That was how things were. He just wanted to say good-bye.

She was standing behind the counter when he went into Snows', tidy in her white shirtwaist and brown twill skirt. When she glanced his way, her large brown eyes grew soft and she smiled her awkward, beautiful smile.

"Hello, Emma," he said. "I thought you might be gone by now."

"Hello, Arthur. I've postponed Seattle for a while."

"Because of the fire?"

"They lost all of their summer clothes. They've got no storage space in the house on account of renting rooms, so Millie had everything in trunks out in the barn. I'm going to make them up new things. And there's to be a Grange Fair, the usual spring fair, I guess, except there'll be a raffle to raise money to help rebuild the barn. I've got a quilt half done that I want to finish off and give. Harry's going to be busy cleaning up the mess and starting the rebuilding, so they need me in the store."

"I came to say good-bye," he said, having a little trouble shifting gears so fast.

"Now you don't need to—not for a while." She looked pleased that it was so—so he dived headfirst into deep waters.

"I was wondering," he said, "if you'd like to come out and see my ranch."

"I'd like to."

"Would Sunday be all right?"

"Sunday would be fine. I could come after church."

"I don't attend church."

"So I've noticed. I don't mind going to church alone, or with the Snows."

"I'll give you some dinner, then, though it won't be much."

"I don't need much."

129

"I'll see you Sunday, then."

"Yes. Did you need anything today?" She glanced around at the canned goods on the shelves, the pickle barrel, the rope coils and boots hanging from the rafters.

He didn't need a thing. "You could sell me a pound of coffee," he said.

She measured it, ground it, tied it up in a bag with string.

After he'd paid, he held out his hand to shake hers, wanting to touch her. She clasped it willingly, he thought.

"The fire was awful," she said. "It gave me nightmares last night. But I liked being in the bucket brigade."

When she let his hand go, he wished she'd kept it longer. "How's Harry doing about the buggy?" It had hurt Arthur to see that buggy burn, its skeleton outlined with flames, a blazing chariot that in half an hour was a pile of ash.

"He's so glad the house and store didn't catch, he hasn't said a word."

"Any news about how it started?"

"Millie was out tending a sore udder on the cow with the new calf. She came back in the house for hot water, leaving the lamp on a shelf. When she went back, it was broken in the hay and the fire had started."

"Cow maybe was startled by a rat, or bumped the stable wall, or flipped her rope against it. They're jumpy when they've got a hurt place or a new calf—or both."

"Millie was heartsick last night, thinking it was her fault, but Harry's finally got her to see it was an accident."

Her look said to him—life can throw terrible things at a person, can't it? His answering look said—it surely can.

"Well, I look forward to Sunday, then," he said. "Do you know how to get to my place?" He wanted to draw her a map or give her minute, detailed directions including every rock and tree, but a look in her eyes warned him off—I got here from Warwick, it said. I can make my way.

"Don't worry. I'll find it."

He couldn't make the talk stretch out any longer, so he had to go away.

130

Emma's step was springy on her way to Arthur's after church. She'd realized, as Mr. Brill droned on, that from fighting the fire and working in the store, she had made a place for herself. She knew just about everyone seated around her, and they knew her. She knew what patent medicines they used, what day their favorite magazines came in, and how they liked their meat cut, with lots of fat, or not. They knew she'd come out probably to marry Arthur Smollett and that it hadn't worked out, but they hadn't held it against her. They had accepted her on her own terms—they'd let her in.

Sonny Snow, in his best knickers, was sailing a cardboard boat in the runoff that filled the ditch next to the road, killing time till dinner and trying to stay clean.

"Hello, Sonny," she called.

He gave her a shy smile and waved his hand without removing it from his pocket, flapping the whole side-bottom of his jacket at her. He was her friend. He liked the well-traveled lemon drops she'd brought from the big glass jar in Neilson's store, glassy yellow candy on the outside with sour-sweet liquid centers that made the mouth juices run. Seeing Sonny, she thought, that's what I want, a boy like that, no matter how much bother Millie says children are. A husband was only a husband, but a child didn't care if you were pretty or smart or up on the latest fashions. A child loved you for life, the way she'd loved Pa. The past tense gave her pain. She wondered if she'd ever hear from him again.

Then, she saw him. He was walking along the street toward her. The clothes were different, but from a distance it was Pa's size and form, his walk and features. Her knees got watery and she thought—what will I do? He's come to take me away from here, to make me go back to Warwick!

The figure came closer and the prominent nose and large dark eyes were almost Pa's—but not quite. It was someone else, and her disappointment and relief were deep.

"How do you do?" said the man, stopping and raising his hat. "You must be the Miss Howe I've heard about, who came to visit Arthur Smollett and helped fight the fire the other night. My wife does most of our storing, so I haven't had the chance to meet you. I'm Jason Parsons, and I'd like to welcome you, belat-

131

edly, to North Falls. I know Arthur through the Odd Fellows—one of our best members. I hope you'll take to this place."

"Thank you," Emma stammered, accepting Mr. Parson's offered hand. She remembered seeing him on top of the ladder, a man who reminded her of Pa. Feeling shaky, she continued on her way. Is this going to keep on happening? she thought, remembering the ghost at the train station the night she'd arrived. Am I going to see Pa everywhere I look for the rest of my life?

The town ended and the shaggy firs crowded down to the edges of the road, dwarfing the traveler. She felt even smaller than usual surrounded by these Western woods and mountains, close, high, rugged. Harry had mentioned mountain lions and bears, as though they were common. Indians lived here, too, not in villages or teepees, but around and about. Some stayed in the woods in cabins they'd built, hunting and fishing. This place wasn't like Vermont. Helping Millie behind the counter, she'd seen customers come into the store wearing guns, not carrying a rifle for deer or a shotgun for ducks, but actually wearing side arms.

She swung off the narrow road onto Arthur's trail. Harry had said, "You'll see it, about three miles out of town, off to the right. It's between a big fir stump and a good sized oak that's still got its leaves." Actually, the oak had lost most of its leaves now, but there was a brown carpet on the ground, the brown a dead, flat color that soaked up the light till it disappeared, giving no light back. She sniffed the sourness of rotting oak leaves.

Gradually the trail started to rise, climbing to Arthur's valley. The dense evergreens cast a heavy, cold shade. Her stomach tightened when she thought of being with Arthur and seeing his ranch for the first time. Millie had let her bake a cake to bring—she didn't like to come to dinner empty-handed—and helped her pack it in a box to carry with a handle made of cloth-wrapped string. Applesauce cake with brown sugar icing, not such a much, just made with what Millie happened to have on hand.

She scrambled up the last steep part of the trail to the ridge top and set down her cake to rest her fingers. She couldn't see Arthur's place through the thick trees, but she could smell

132

smoke. Over to the north and west she could hear, very faintly on the wind now and again, the buzz of a saw. Hal's mill, she thought. Must be a rush job if he were working on a Sunday.

The trail entered a tall pine forest where the sun slanted through in streaks and the ground turned quiet underfoot with needles. She stopped to take in the rays of light, sensing a holy place, remembering other moments: the lady slippers blossoming out of the ashes of the forest fire, a sunrise over Stannard Mountain after an ice storm where branches, bushes, and the sweep of fields flamed red and glittered. The light sifting through the pines was less dramatic, but it gave her the same feeling of awe and oneness. Being with people could give that same feeling, briefly, with Ma in her childhood sometimes, with Pa before Paul, with Paul before he went back to Quebec—with Arthur before she'd met him. She had to have that feeling about a person if they were to be friends.

She strode along steadily. The trail, pleasant walking, wound east and north, down and into the valley, never dropping too fast or twisting too far. As she emerged into the edge of sumac, blueberry, and privet, she looked north and saw she'd come in the easy way. The ridge in the distance was steeper, bluish-green with firs, brushy with patches of deciduous treetops. The whole ridge looked tender from a distance, all those hard branches soft as fur, as though you could stroke your hand over their purplish gray, what the ladies' pattern books called mauve, whereas in truth to bushwhack through that woods would tear a hiker into bleeding shreds.

She ducked under a grapevine, and there it was. The cabin. The barn. The ranch. Arthur.

She had the advantage of seeing him first. He was busy hauling something in a barrow, dirt, it seemed, over to a double row of cold frames near the cabin. The beds were raised and enclosed by thick slabs of tree trunk—what a deal of sweat and skinned knuckles it must have cost to haul those slabs, she thought. She watched as he shoveled out the wooden barrow. She heard the thump of the spade against the back, watched as he lifted one side of the barrow off the flat bottom and scraped along the edges and into the corners, then tipped the barrow and knocked it with the spade to get the rest. No sense carrying

133

back when you'd meant to bring, hefting the same burden twice. It was how Pa would have done it. She swallowed, straightened her skirt, smoothed her hair, and walked forward with her cake into the clearing.

Her approach was so quiet that he didn't hear her till she was all the way across the wide yard and standing by the barrow as he arranged the dirt—compost, actually—in the new bed.

"Hello, Arthur," she said.

Taken by surprise, he was struck by her low voice and the broad *a* she gave his name. Most folks he knew out here said *hey*, or *howdy*, not *hello*. *Hél ló, Aáh-tha*. She sounded like everything about Somerville that he hated and held most dear, all he'd sought to get away from and could never escape, no more than he could obliterate the tracings marked on his mind long before memory, as he had lain in his cradle absorbing how the sunlight came in the window just so, smelling rice pudding, hearing in the other room his mother greeting the postman at the door. *Hél ló, Aáh-tha*.

"Well, Emma. You're in good time."

She liked the way those two teeth at the side overlapped, peeping out from beneath his moustache when he smiled. It was a sandy moustache, she thought—not really blond.

"It was an easy walk."

"How are you, then?"

"Well. And you?"

"Working on a scheme, as you can see. I hope to use the heat of compost in decay to give these beds an early start."

She saw small cabbages, lettuce, beets, spinach—tiny green sprouts, all as clearly defined by just two pin-sized leaves as they would be full grown and ready to pick.

"You have all these already!"

"Yes, but it's hard to tell if they'll take until they're bigger. I have to be careful not to overdo the compost. Burn these sprouters out."

"I'd never have thought even to try."

"You have to have the climate. Back in Somerville, everything's a solid chunk of ice still."

"You get letters?"

"Not to speak of. My mother used to write, but I guess she

134

gave up when I didn't answer, but for Easter and Christmas. I'm not a good correspondent."

"You did pretty well to me."

The overlapping teeth winked at her again. "I was under no obligation. And even then I seem to recall some complaints—that I was too slow, that you'd been looking for a letter."

She wished she could say it wasn't so, that she hadn't clung to his letters as to a lifeline. She wasn't happy about that time and how she'd seen him then, and she looked away from him, in the direction of the northern ridge, but really at nothing.

"Sometimes you'd write two to my one, and always twice as long," he said, having to press his advantage, needing to.

"Only because I'd nothing better to do and love to write."

"Is that so?" The smile became a grin, and she didn't like it, did not like standing there in her good dress, holding her gift of cake. Two minutes together and already they were at odds, she thought. She hunted around for something to wound him with.

"So this is your ranch. I imagined it bigger."

"It's more than enough for one man to farm. I've had to hire Martin just to keep even."

"It seems small after ours—three hundred acres."

He shrugged.

"That's hay, timber, orchard, and pasture. Summers we have a hired hay crew going all June, most of July. Frenchmen down from Canada." Everything was veiled, but she was not only telling him she came from a bigger farm—she was telling him about Paul, that he, Arthur Smollett, was not the first or only, nor should he think he was. Arthur couldn't translate *hay crew* into *a lover named Paul.* He could only sense he was being put in his place.

"Well, this is plenty enough for me. Seven years ago, it was just a thick, wooded swamp. So I measure in terms of yards, not acres."

She nodded, respecting his achievement. Now that she'd reminded him that she came from more acres—even if she did write more letters—she felt restored to balance, as though they were just about even.

"I'd like to leave my cake somewhere."

135

"Come along," he said. "You can set it in the cabin. It was nice of you to bring it."

The front door was heavy creosoted planks. The inside, when she peeked, was surprisingly neat—not neat for company but from habit.

"Let me tour you around while the sun shines. Then later you can inspect my housekeeping."

His step was eager as he led the way through the kitchen garden, past the toolshed, outhouse, hen house, barn, and bin of compost. Out beyond were his vegetable gardens, fruit trees, berry bushes. Everything was fenced: turkey wire at the bottom, wire strands above, brushy branches woven into the top. She was impressed to think he'd done all of this alone, but sensed that, like her people, he'd view any praise as fulsome— "Praise to your face is half disgrace."

"Fences to keep out the cows?" She noticed a couple-three Jerseys grazing loose on dead grass out among the stumps. One looked to be with calf.

"And the critters. The brush at the top is for the deer. Lots of rabbits and woodchucks, too. I had a dog, but he died. I'll be getting a new one before my new crops come up in earnest. Your folks keep dogs?"

He looked straight at her, so she knew it was more than a casual question. She thought—blue eyes aren't so bad.

"We kept one called Hunter till I was fifteen, when he died. Now we just have a big old tomcat, to patrol the barn. A white cat, hard to spot him in the snow."

"I need a dog to patrol the gardens. Martin and Annie have a new litter of pups. Maybe you'd help me pick one out."

"I'd like to," she said, pleased.

"I thought to get a dog when my old one died, but decided to wait. Dogs are funny creatures and get loyal to one person fast. I thought—it would be better for a new dog to know us both. That was back then, of course."

"Of course," she said. "That was thoughtful of you, back then. But I'd be happy to help you pick one out now. Today, even."

Her eager consent was all he needed to make him joyful. He took her arm and they walked back toward the cabin where he hoped his dinner would be fit to eat. His body, which had felt

136

bony and hard to her when they'd first met, now seemed warm and solid. As she surveyed his ranch, she thought that there was certainly plenty to do here, enough to keep more than one person busy. What the place needed was some flowers.

At the end of the afternoon, Arthur walked her back to the oak at the end of the trail, and before they parted, they approached each other, as if by a common prompting, to get the awkwardness of a first kiss out of the way. They edged up to it like children cautiously tasting a new dish, ready to put down their forks and say phoo at the first sign of a piece of loathsome onion. But the dish passed—Emma felt a spark and Arthur a whole shower of them—and each walked home in a mood of high self-congratulation. Arthur whistled "The Battle Hymn of the Republic." Emma sang to herself: "White wings, that never grow weary, that carry me cheerily over the sea. / Night comes, I long for you, dear one, so put on your white wings and sail home to me."

North Falls watched them court. She went out to his ranch with her quilt in a basket after church the next Sunday.

"Get a lot of squares done?" Millie asked slyly. Emma held up the pile to show that, yes, she had.

On Wednesday, driving by with his team, Bert saw Arthur, who never took an afternoon off, hiking with her out to the old "gold" mine in Iron Mountain, the mine that turned out to have a mother lode of pyrite worth a bit less than nothing.

"There's good camping here," Arthur told her on the hike. "Skiing, snowshoeing, and fishing, too. Hunting, for those that hunt."

"I take it you don't hunt?"

He looked uncomfortable. "I mind shooting animals though I find I don't mind the meat. It's an inconsistency, a flaw in my character. If you benefit from the one, you should be able to do the other."

"Most buy from a butcher and never give the matter a thought," she said. It didn't seem important. She might have worried about it back in her "bloodroot" period when she was trying to iron all the wrinkles out of the world. But not now.

Obviously it was important to him, for he went on with it.

"It's different with a trout or a chicken. I don't *like* killing one, but I can do it, all right. But I don't want to shoot a deer. I tried once with Hal and I couldn't do it."

He looked very uncomfortable indeed, and she became aware that she was listening to a confession. He was ashamed of not being a hunter and he wanted her to know his weakness. She remembered the thumbless hand of the conductor on the train the day she left home, the "dues" he had paid. Her seatmate had made some remark about mutilation no longer being necessary to manhood. Arthur wasn't exactly talking about mutilation, but he was showing her a fear that had him doubting himself.

"You don't have to shoot anything," she said. "It makes no nevermind to me. It doesn't matter."

He turned away from her, almost angrily, before he replied, and she realized that her being soothing was not going to help.

"It does to me," he said.

On Saturday Arthur couldn't borrow Harry's burned-up buggy, so they took the train to Everett and dined in style at the hotel on Dungeness crab and a bottle of home brew Arthur provided through a sidewalk purchase.

"The Spanish War was a bad one," he told her. "After the *Maine* was blown up, Spain agreed to McKinley's every condition. Things should have ended there."

"Oh, no," she said. "Dewey had to take Manila."

"So now we're stuck with Roosevelt, the 'big game hunter,' " he said scornfully. "McKinley was a better man."

The forty proof home brew was making her mellow, so she let that pass. Over dessert he told her, "When my father died, I was twelve. He'd been very tired for a couple of days, so he went upstairs to take a nap. He never woke up. All my life, I've been afraid I'd die in my sleep."

On the way home on the train, she nestled against him a little bit drunk.

"I was in love with a French Canadian once," she told him. "Paul Goddard, who came to help with the hay when I was nineteen."

"You know Bert Brown's daughter, Elva," he said. "I was sort of in love with her."

She felt soothed by his admission, having already figured it out.

"I'll tell you about Paul sometime," she said, and fell asleep on his shoulder.

Nobody had ever fallen asleep on his shoulder before. He felt honored and protective, as though a bluebird had alighted on his finger to feed from his palm. Whoever this Paul was, he couldn't have been much.

Emma finished knitting the green muffler, and when Arthur said it was the nicest one he'd ever had, she went ahead with a sweater to match. Holding the back against his back, to see if it was long enough and time to decrease for the sleeves, was an intimate pleasure to her. She liked the shape and feel of his back through its coarse blue cotton shirt, faded with many washings. She wanted him to dress well, in strong colors, and stay warm wearing something she had made herself.

Arthur gave her the gift he'd had in his pocket when she arrived and never gotten to give. It was a piece of scrimshaw showing a big tree surrounded by flowers on the ground and birds in the sky. Even without his telling her, she knew it was a copper beech.

"I used to pass one every day on the way to school," he said. "I loved that tree. I used to imagine I could move into it and live there."

He was proud to give Emma something beautiful he'd carved himself, something that would appeal to her aesthetic sense and show her that he was more than just a mud farmer. When she admired his craftsmanship, he felt like a million bucks.

Martha Landis invited them to "a little supper," for which she killed, cleaned, plucked, stuffed, and cooked a goose. She made gravy, five dozen fritters, roasted a big butternut squash, stewed some dried plums, and baked a peach cobbler the size of a dresser top. She knew she could outcook any such sprig as Emma, and she wanted to be sure both Emma and Arthur knew it. They came away convinced. Nearly back to Snows', Emma

139

still felt as stuffed as the goose, and was surprised, in the middle of a more than tentative kiss, by a big burp.

"Oh, dear," she wailed, humiliated—"I'm sorry. How awful for you."

Arthur laughed till he had to go behind a tree and pee. She disappeared into the bushes, too, and then felt better.

"I threw up in school once," he said, "all over the floor, my school pants, and my spelling paper."

"It must have been awful."

"Well, I didn't think it was much fun. And throwing up's much worse than a burp."

She put the ends of her shawl up over her scarlet face. "Don't remind me. Oh, I'm so ashamed."

Just then they ran into Harry, coming back from dropping the evening mail at the train.

"What's the joke, folks?" he said, seeing Arthur laughing and Emma hiding.

Arthur was about to tell when he saw Emma's stricken face.

"A private matter," he said.

"I didn't think anything was private in North Falls," said Harry, who loved gossip.

"Well, this time it is. Good evening to you, Harry."

Harry had the grace to go into the house, and Arthur, suddenly serious and full of courage, said, "I think we should get married."

Love wasn't the issue, not love as he'd imagined it, but this was a woman who knew kale from pigweed when they were both only one inch high and who could hike all afternoon in the rain without complaining.

She liked him. She respected him. The spark had started a flame in the kindling, and she wanted a family.

"All right," she said.

XVIII

LORD HAVE mercy, I'm married, Emma thought as she heard the words "man and wife." On the surface there was happiness, but it rested on a layer of loss: none of her family here, Howe with its stylish *e* traded for Smollett with its redundant *t*, the possibility of Seattle for the reality of North Falls. And to offset all of that, only Arthur, who was looking handsome but nervous as he paid Mr. Brill.

Hal kissed the bride. Millie kissed the groom. The Snows had them in for a little spread of sandwiches and homemade wine, and then it was eight o'clock and time to go back to the cabin. Emma hugged Sonny, who liked it, and Buddy, who squirmed, and said she'd see them soon.

Arthur didn't have a whole lot to say on the way back. She supposed he was worn out by the day, too, and also balancing his losses against his gains. She was the gain, she realized, and right now she didn't feel up to the job. She felt as though both of them had surrendered to a design greater than their own. They'd been fooled into thinking they'd chosen each other, but really life had chosen them, insisted that they step up, pay their money, and take their chances in the next game.

"I'll let you off from chores tonight as it's our honeymoon," Arthur joked when they got to the cabin. She suspected he wanted some time to himself and was glad to give it. She knew his cabin well by now, but wandered into the bedroom, picking things up and putting them down as though the whole place were unfamiliar. She was that jittery about making love with Arthur that she would have welcomed a Bible, so she could

141

read, not just recite from memory, that "Love is not resentful. Love bears all things, believes all things, hopes all things, endures all things." Arthur, of course, didn't keep a Bible, and hers was still buried at the bottom of her trunk.

The next best thing to a Bible was his dictionary, where he seemed to have tucked two folded papers. One said: "Homestead certificate number 6660, Application 16260. According to an Act of Congress on 20 May 1862 to secure Homesteads to actual settlers on the public domain . . ." *Arthur Smollett* was written in the blank above. *William McKinley* was signed down below.

The other paper was a clipping: "President McKinley Assassinated at an Exposition in Buffalo," the headline read, and in the opening paragraph she found the name of the assassin, Leon Czolgosz. Of course, she thought, in 1901—how could I forget so fast? Though why should I remember that man's name when what he did was murder a president? We should all forget him. Better that Arthur Smollett be remembered for doing something useful—clearing his homestead, building a house, and raising food.

Righteous indignation about Leon Czolgosz put her in a better frame of mind, and she looked around the crowded room, where her sewing machine, valise, and trunk were huddled in a corner, jostling for space. How do I fit in? she thought. What will I be remembered for, I who've neither cleared, nor planted, nor built? She looked at the bed. She had felt passion with Paul, lying in the dark with him for an hour at a time, never completing the act because of fear and the powerful presence of Pa. Now she had traveled over the curve of the world, so many miles that nobody knew where she was. It was like taking her book to the top of the apple tree where Ma's voice couldn't reach her and call her to clean all the staircases with a brush and a dustpan. Here, in this hidden place, she could look at this bed and imagine making love in it, naked and warm by firelight from the other room. Making love many times till she slept pregnant in the bed. Her labor and delivery of a child in it. That child would be her claim to be remembered. It's what I came for, she thought boldly, and it's foolish to pretend otherwise.

The sooner, the better. So when Arthur came back from the barn, she was still nervous but ready to want him.

Arthur, nervous as well, stopped at the outhouse on his way. If he was going to perform as a husband—and he hoped he was—he had to empty his bladder first.

When he walked into his private bedroom, he was surprised to find it occupied. He was also surprised that Emma had undressed to her chemise and petticoat—but pleased at what he misread as a greater sign of readiness than it really was. This won't take long, he thought. He eagerly peeled off his shirt, boots, and trousers, hoping that his underwear looked passably clean—the flies tended to get grimy.

He was surprised by the robustness of her arms and shoulders. She might be small but she was sturdy, made strong, no doubt, by work on her father's three-hundred-acre farm. He remembered how delicate she had looked when he first saw her in the Snows' kitchen, yet how formidable in her carefully matched outfit and her thick hair pinned up high as it still was now. Miss Emma Howe of Warwick, Vermont.

"Don't you want to take down your hair?" he asked, his voice husky.

She removed the pins and the brown waves cascaded down, a fur shawl over her shoulders. It made him feel better to see her look younger and more intimately revealed.

"Stand up," he said urgently, wanting to press her against his body and have her feel how ready he was for her.

She stood, though she didn't quite want to because of an echo of some other such request that she had not liked at all. She didn't understand why he wanted her to stand. She thought he looked a bit ridiculous in his underwear but might look worse without it. She wished for darkness. He kissed her, and she wanted to fall into the kiss and forget herself but couldn't because he seemed rough and in a hurry. The hairs of his moustache, freshly trimmed for the wedding, scraped the delicate membranes of her nose.

"You're lovely," he whispered, kissing her again, smoothing his hands down her shoulders, waist, hips. He laid her back across the bed, undoing his buttons. He meant to go slow, to have everything about their first lovemaking be gentle and

143

adoring, but as he kissed her again, he got caught in the rushing current of his own need. Everything about her—the way she smelled of soap and roses, the way her skin was silkier and softer than anything he had ever felt, the way she returned his kiss—whirled his senses faster and faster till he couldn't hold back. He raised her petticoat, groped, and little by little thrust himself in. It wasn't easy—with the Jamaican woman and Betty Pilchuck it had been easy—but of course for them it hadn't been a first time. Then he stopped noticing and only felt. His borders blurred as they blended with Emma's. His pleasure was so intense as to be almost painful.

Lying on her with his face buried in her shoulder, he thought at first of nothing, sensing only a great release. When awareness returned, he guessed the deflowering couldn't have been too bad for her—at least it was rapid. Then he nearly dozed off, lulled by the warmth and softness of her body, till he felt her stir and realized she wanted to be free.

"Am I too heavy?" he asked and lifted himself off and to one side. By the time he saw her face, the tears that had sprung into her eyes had been reabsorbed leaving no trace, except that her eyes were huge and solemn.

"Are you all right?" he asked.

"I guess," she said, though there was a fiery place between her legs as though she'd been burned.

"It'll be easier next time," he said.

"I hope so."

He pulled on a pair of pants. "I'll make tea," he said, needing to so something. "My tea's better than my coffee."

There was blood on her petticoat. She winced when she sat across from him at the table.

"I'm sorry," he said. "It's because you're new to it. Are you really hurt?"

She saw the worry in his face. If she sat perfectly still, she was not uncomfortable, but she was terribly disappointed. It hadn't been like this before, she wanted to say. But she also knew that Paul's face had never worn this look of tender concern. How did Paul know to do the things he did, to make her body rejoice? She hardly knew any French, and she had never been able to ask him or really wanted to know. But now it was clear that Paul

144

had known how to make love to her and that Arthur, her husband, did not. Paul had left her. Arthur had married her. Arthur had said she was lovely, and then done this painful thing to her. Now he was offering her cream and sugar, and she saw the naked need for reassurance in his face. None of it made much sense. She thought: it can only get better, for it can't get worse. I know more about this than he does and I've got to find a way to teach him, because this won't do.

"Next time let's not be so quick," she said.

XIX

Daffodil pushed one final time and the calf slid out like a grape popped out of its skin. It was a heifer, well formed, already scrambling to totter on its brand-new legs.

"Hey, there!" said Arthur in welcome.

It was close to midnight and he had been in the barn since supper, but he didn't mind. He'd never gotten tired of seeing animals born. He conceded that it might not be the best method of reproduction. Some plants could scatter seeds, send out runners, and form roots on broken branches as well. But an animal's struggle to bring forth its young satisfied his sense of how things should, and sometimes did, work: effort was rewarded.

Watching the calf start to suckle, he remembered seeing a colt stillborn to a dying mother when he first had come out to homestead. He'd still been a city boy then and the event had affected him—the mare's effort had made no difference. And of course human effort was often evil or misguided. After the *Maine* was blown up in Havana Harbor, the yellow press had whipped the people up and nothing would do but that Dewey must fight at Manila and Roosevelt must storm up San Juan Hill and into the White House. Long over, that whole business still continued to plague him—he didn't know why. All his North Falls neighbors knew that Arthur Smollett didn't like T.R. or the war with Spain. He'd told them enough times. Daffodil had produced a fine calf, Arthur thought, but his pleasure somehow got mixed up with his hatred of Roosevelt. The big game hunter, a pose that celebrated violence. It was false, and he held dishonesty the worst human failing. Rosebud, he thought, we'll name the new calf Rosebud, after the President. It'll be a joke between Em and me.

When he went into the house and told her, she was mixing bread sponge, which she would set to rise overnight. Fresh bread tomorrow—not like his corn bread-hardtack days. He washed at the sink and got into bed, tired but gratified by the day and its events. He needed only his wife to complete it.

"You almost done?"

"In a minute."

He heard the soothing thunk of her wooden spoon against the sides of the crockery bowl. They'd been married close to a week now, and he was surprised at how accustomed he already was. Glad for her work. Pleased to see her at the end of the day, to tell her his news. At first she was shy with him. Eating meals, she'd chatter as if her life depended on keeping him entertained. Her monthly period had come the day after the wedding, interrupting the honeymoon and embarrassing her though he'd tried to reassure her that he knew all about such things—it wasn't as if he'd never had a sister. Em had had some restless nights, had woken with strange dreams, and he'd worried that she missed her home, family, and comforts. He, on the other hand, already slept better with her in the bed.

"It's late," he called, "come along now." He hadn't made love to her since the wedding day, but her period was over now—he'd asked her at supper—and he was eager for her. It would be better this time.

The light went out in the other room to a little huff of breath. He heard her rustle out of her clothes and made out, though there was only moonlight to see by, the curve of her arm as she reached to hang her dress on its peg. She used to toss it over a chair back, but he'd cleared half the pegs for her and she'd changed her habit, hung her dress up on his account, because he didn't like clothes lying about on the furniture. He loved her for that—it wasn't easy to learn new ways. He hoped she was happy that she'd come to North Falls. She hadn't slept so restless last night. She'd told him she liked warming her cold feet on his warm ones.

He heard the click of her hairpins on the dresser top and the flutter of her nightdress as it fell around her like a jib settling on

147

a boom. Her bare feet padded across the wooden floorboards. The sound got muffled as she crossed the braided rug she'd put down, made by her ma, brought in her trunk. He wanted her feet in bed with him.

"Are you going to be all night out there?" he said.

"Only half the night." Her "half," sounding like the "baa" of a sheep, made him smile.

He listened to her clean her teeth and brush her hair. A jar lid unwound and was screwed back on. At last the mattress moved as she climbed in beside him. She smelled of roses, some sort of salve she rubbed on her hands to offset chapping. He felt as if he'd been waiting for hours and reached for her. He wasn't afraid of her tonight, not worried that he might not be able to perform. He kissed her and squeezed her breast.

In the middle of the kiss, she took his hand, loosened its hold, and flicked his fingers against the nipple, lightly back and forth. All right, he thought, if that's what you want. The nipple surprised him by standing up under his touch, hard as an unripe blueberry. Trying to please her, he gave the other nipple the same treatment while kissing her again. He felt her body relax during the kiss and was pleased, ready to get on with things. He reached for the hem of her nightgown, but again her hand took his and he found she was licking, then sucking, two of his fingers. He was reminded of Elva licking her finger and putting it against his catbriar scratch in the backroom of the Odd Fellows' Hall, and he didn't like the association, didn't trust what Emma was doing to him. He didn't want Elva, a silly flirt, and Emma, his wife, mixed up in his head. She kept at it. He had to admit it was a pleasure, if a bit excessive, but he wasn't sure he liked having Emma take the lead. What was going on here, anyway? He was starting to feel as frustrated as a person with a sneeze coming on who couldn't bring it to fruition—he didn't want to wait. But even more, he didn't like her taking over, didn't like her asking for this dubious, maybe even unnatural, attention. He remembered the Jamaican woman and Betty Pilchuck and thought: that's a whore's trick.

"Where'd you learn that?" he said gruffly.

There was a long silence before she answered. "From Paul."

148

He heard his own sharp intake of breath. "Paul. You were going to tell me about him, but you never did."

Silence. He reclaimed his hand and she let him.

"Who was Paul?"

"He came down from Quebec one summer. Pa hired him to help us with the hay. I used to meet him, evenings."

She was speaking so low he could barely hear her, but he knew he'd heard correctly. "I thought I was the first," he said.

"You were. Are. You know that."

"In a manner of speaking. But I'm not the first you've loved or wanted."

"That's true."

"Why didn't you marry him?" he asked, biting back the rest of the sentence that formed in his mind—if you loved him so much?

"I told you, he was French Canadian, a Catholic—a Canuck. My family look down on Canucks, all of Warwick does. And the one time I went to his aunt and uncle's house—well, I didn't fit in with them, everyone rattling away in French and laughing at jokes I couldn't understand—probably at me. Eating blood sausage, all oozy on the plate—I couldn't choke down even one bite. And small white onions pickled with red pepper—they gave me one and everyone hooted when it made my eyes water and my nose run, it was so hot. And then, of course, he went back home at the end of the summer. It was a bad time for me when he left. I couldn't eat or sleep, but I had to because Pa had his eye on me every minute. I felt as though I'd die and I had to get out of the house. That was when I got my shop. It saved my life. I escaped into the village, and the shop occupied my thoughts."

It was his turn to be quiet. "You should have told me. I look for truth in people. That's what I look for most, courage and truth. You didn't tell me."

"I did tell you, on the train coming back from Everett."

"Not the whole of it."

"How could I tell you all of it? Pa cursed me because of Paul and because I wanted to come out here. I left home against his will." He couldn't see her face, but he heard her voice quaver. "I couldn't tell you. I was afraid you wouldn't love me."

149

"Love isn't the point." He thought—women always clutter up the issue with love.

"It is for me. It's much more than courage or honesty. I haven't asked if you've been with others. You mentioned Elva, but you as much as said she wasn't important, and I believed you. If you've been with others, I don't want to know."

He took a deep breath. "I have. Two. Some time ago, and not good women."

"You didn't love them?"

"Of course not," he said impatiently.

"Then it doesn't matter."

"But you did love Paul. You grieved when he went away. It did matter and you didn't tell me. Now you want me to make love to you his way. No doubt so you can imagine you're with him again."

"That's not so! I was only nineteen when it happened, six years ago—it's over. But I do want—I do want to feel about you the way I felt about him. I want our being in bed together to be —a joy to me." She said this very low, but he heard and was surprised. He'd hoped not to hurt her again. He hadn't thought about her wanting pleasure.

"Damn your Paul. I wish there'd never been a Paul."

"But you've been with others. You said—"

"Not good women, Emma. Not women who were wives. I married you because you were a good woman."

"And now you think I'm not."

He was at a loss. She sounded bitter, betrayed, but *he* was the one who had been betrayed. "You lied to me by not telling me the whole of it. I think people ought to treat each other right, but you didn't. So I'll wish you good night."

He got out of bed and went into the other room, slamming the door behind him, shutting her out of his turbulent thoughts. He yanked an old horse blanket off a peg by the front door and threw it on the floor by the stove, then lay down on it with a coat over him for a cover. He was breathing hard. He shut Emma out of his mind, but he couldn't sleep. What rose up in his memory was the hunting trip with Hal when he couldn't kill the deer. He'd had it in his sights. He had drawn a bead on it. He hadn't been able to pull the trigger.

I'll get a rifle, he thought, and go out tomorrow. I'll get it this time. He wanted to stalk alone in the woods for as long as it took, follow his prey, canny and quiet for hours, then catch up with it, sight along the barrel, this time complete the act with the explosion, blood, and death. He'd been avoiding it for years, but now he wanted to do it. I've got to do it, he thought, and he went to sleep with his plans made.

He was still asleep on the floor when someone knocked in the morning. Martin, he thought, waking with a start.

"Hold on," he called. In a hurry, he put away his makeshift bedding and went into the bedroom, where he pulled on a pair of pants. Then he opened the front door.

"Overslept, Arthur?" Martin grinned.

"Daffodil dropped her calf," Arthur said.

"I saw. When'd she have it?"

"Close to midnight."

"That's no excuse for late sleeping," Martin said. "But a honeymoon is." He laughed and set down the milk. "Cleaning the hen house today, isn't that it? I came equipped."

"That's it," said Arthur, who had forgotten. No hunting. Chicken shit instead.

"Might as well do it early and get it over. Or as early as you can manage. Honeymooners move slow, ain't that so?" He nudged Arthur with his elbow. "Ain't it? Ain't it, Arthur?"

"I guess that's about right," said Arthur, because he had to.

Martin went out to get started on the hen house, and Arthur built up the fire for breakfast. He was blowing on the kindling when Emma came in. She was dressed and braided while he was still in his bare feet and pants. He felt the disadvantage.

"Letting Martin believe something that's not so—that's a lie, isn't it?" she said, saucy as you please, and then marched out to the privy so he couldn't answer.

He was not a shouting man, and he couldn't shout after her anyway because Martin was in the yard. But he grew plants and he knew how to wait. He waited until she came in.

"Don't you ever talk to me like that again," he said. "You hear?"

151

They ate their breakfast at the same table, in silence, not once meeting each other's gaze. When sunlight glinted on the handle of the silver sugar spoon Millie and Harry had given them for a wedding present, he saw the deer rifle gleam in his imagination.

XX

S HE HADN'T thought he could be so stubborn. She hadn't believed she could be so unhappy. After the first night on the pallet, he'd moved back into the bed, but for two days he hadn't touched her. When she reached out a hand to his turned back, feeling the row of ribs under the waffle cloth of his long johns, he lay rigid until she took her hand away. If their elbows bumped by mistake, he moved toward his side of the mattress. It seemed like two weeks. Last night she had pleaded, "Arthur, talk to me."

"There's nothing to talk about," he'd said.

This morning, instead of inspecting the seedlings growing on his experimental composted bed to see if they could be transplanted to the regular cold frame, she just sat at the breakfast table, not wanting to move. She was supposed to be happy—she was on her honeymoon—but it had turned into a disaster.

Yesterday, he'd been gone all day and had returned long after suppertime. When she'd asked where he'd been, he'd said, "I can't abide having to tell you my every move. Having to ask permission."

"It's not permission. It's only information."

"That's not how it seems to me."

Today he'd been gone before she woke up and she had no idea where he was. She didn't know if transplanting the seedlings was what she should do, didn't know whether to plan any dinner, or supper, for that matter. She thought there was no point in staying, not like this. The marriage was a failure, and she was a failure—an ugly failure. All her interest in the gar-

153

dens, orchard, and berry patches—she had been planning to prune before the spring came on—had disappeared. He was civil, but as cold as a house shut up in winter. He fried the breakfast bacon and passed the pepper, but apart from the amenities of please and thank you, he didn't talk. His presence in the cabin was like the violence of ice.

She'd started having nightmares. Night before last she'd dreamed that Pa had died and that all the women in her family —Ma, the aunts, her sisters—had died as well in some vague, mysterious way. She had woken choked with tears and sobs, her body distressed by the powerful illusions of her mind, the word *alone* repeating in her ears. Ever since that dream, she'd felt no connection to Arthur's cabin. Everything in it was strange—his chairs, his dishes. This is not my place, she said to herself—*not my place, not my place.*

She yearned for home, and the letter from Ma, when Hal brought it by, catching her still at the table at nine o'clock, seemed an answer to that yearning. Arthur might reject her and scoff at love, but the people at home hadn't died in her dream. They still loved her and had felt her need for them even though she hadn't written to them of her trouble. She smoothed the letter from home with her fingers several times. Just touching it made her less unhappy. It was proof that she was loved and might give her the courage to find an answer to the question that had been haunting her—what can I do now? Where can I go?

"Want me to go away while you read it, Emma?" Hal asked.

She'd forgotten about Hal. "No, no," she said. "Sit down."

He sat and eyed her with curiosity. She supposed she must look strange—not dressed yet (lazy), wearing her wrapper (slovenly), her hair loose down her back (wanton).

"Did you want Arthur?" she asked, needing to summon the presence of a husband to legitimize the scene. "He went out somewhere early. I don't know where."

"He's gone to get a deer, borrowed my gun and would have borrowed me except I've got a load of lumber to see to, I'll take it down on the train Monday, it's almost ready."

"Oh!" she said, yanked by this information out of her self concern into a brief awareness of the depth of Arthur's distress.

154

He's gone off to test himself, she thought—he's braver than I thought. Then she tore open the letter, raced through it, and forgot her admiration for Arthur's facing his demon.

Pa, a stroke, bed rest, she read. Pa's father had died of a stroke. It was the one illness Pa feared. "He's been very bad," Ma wrote. "I expect he'd be glad if you came."

"Lumber?" she said, foggy, but an idea already forming.

"A load for Seattle, I'm taking it down Monday, want to go down with me and see the sights?"

"Not to Seattle," she said. "But I'll ride with you as far as Everett." Everett was the first stop to home.

"Yes? Why, Emma Smollett, this is good news! I'll count on you, treat you to lunch at the hotel, though you mustn't tell Arthur, he might take it amiss as he's on his honeymoon, can you be ready for the morning train?"

"Yes!" She was happy for the first time in what seemed like years. She'd pack her valise and leave the rest—sewing machine, quilts, she didn't want them, didn't need them, at home she had everything she needed. She hoped for his sake that Arthur did get a deer, but that wouldn't change her plans—she was going home to Pa! Pa, who would never shut her out the way Arthur had done, at least not forever, not if he was so sick, now he would forgive her, surely. Pa didn't need to know anything of what had happened to her here, only that she needed to come home. Pa had always been able to read her heart.

"Well, that's all settled then, I'll come by for you, shall I? Or meet you down to Snows', we'll just run off together and leave Arthur to enjoy his famous deer alone, if he manages to get one, which I doubt, you know he's never got a deer before, serve him right if he gets one now and has to deal with it himself."

"Snows'," she said, again remembering the rest of the world, not just herself. "Oh, my—I'm remembering I told Dee Brown I'd help her can albacore today. I'd best be about it."

She jumped up from the table and dashed into the other room to dress.

"See you Monday," Hal called through the closed bedroom door.

The fish was silvery—gutted, headless, limp. It dripped icy pond water. It and close to forty others had spent the night there in a fine mesh basket to protect them from raccoons.

"Like this," Dee said. She ran a small sharp knife down the spine of the fish before her and lifted out the filet. She turned the fish, her fingers red with cold, and fileted the other side. She slashed a filet in two and dropped the pieces into a pint jar where they just fitted.

"You don't use the dark meat?" Emma asked.

"The hogs eat it. Strong and oily don't bother them."

The baby, Frieda, slept in her cradle in the corner. Saturday and no school—Dee's boys were down playing at Snows'. Dee shooed Molly and Jane up to the loft with their dolls, since it was raining.

"Come and play, Emma." Molly held her wooden doll out invitingly. Emma realized it was a generous offer—this was the doll that took all the major roles in Molly's games.

"We'll play some later," she promised. "I have to can fish now. I made your mother get a late start."

"I have to can fish, too," said Molly importantly. Emma could see Dee in the child, Dee with thick hair and a thin body, her face unmarked by age and labor. "Come on, Jane," said Molly, and pushed her younger sister toward the ladder, taking the lead much as Emma used to with Anne and Maggie.

"I don't want to can fish," Jane protested.

"Yes, you do," said Molly. "For the winter. It's that or smoke them, and you know we like them better canned." The two girls, in pinafores and long black stockings, climbed to the loft.

"Just what I said to Mr. Brown this morning," Dee remarked. "Little pitchers have big ears."

"Where are Lucy and Elva?" Emma asked, wondering why the two big girls weren't helping their stepmother.

"Gone to Everett. Their grandma, who's their mother's mother, asked them down. She came and raised them for a while after their mother died, till she and Mr. Brown began to scrape on each other. They never did get along."

"A nice change for them," said Emma. She was catching on to how sharp the knife was, how much pressure to apply, how to avoid bones yet not leave any flesh clinging. Dead fish that used

156

to dart quick in the river. Squirming with life one instant, nailed to a slab by knife point the next. A growing tree, a chunk of lifeless wood. Her marriage as good as dead, and right now death might be happening to Pa. She'd be packed tomorrow and Monday would come soon.

Dee haggled the top off a box of salt with her knife, holding the box against her chest. She scooped a spoonful into each jar. "The girls went down at New Year's. Their grandma kept them long enough to spoil them. Bought them new shoes and dresses. When she was sick of them, she sent them back to me. All we heard for weeks was what a sad, poky life we have here on the ranch."

"They might find situations in Everett. Be happier there."

"Lucy can take direction. She could learn to run a typewriting machine or wait on tables at the inn. I expect you've noticed about Elva. All she wants is a man."

Like Arthur, Emma thought, hurt at the idea in spite of herself. When I go, she'll have a clear field. Well, she's welcome to him. "My pa's bad," she told Dee. "I just heard today—it's a stroke. I'm thinking I'll go home to see him."

"That's too bad. Seems like you just got here."

"It's been a long time, to me."

"Your pa could be gone before you arrive."

"Oh, no," said Emma confidently, not wanting to admit that a minute earlier she'd been imagining the same thing. She had to think Pa would be there for her, would hang on until she came.

"It's a long way for a funeral and no comfort to the dead," Dee said. "My ma passed on not too long after I came out here from Tulsa. Answered Mr. Brown's advertisement for a housekeeper when he was a widower and the grandma had gone back to Everett with her nose out of joint. Married him two weeks after. Had one baby and another coming when I heard my ma was dying. I wanted to go, but I couldn't. Bert's people back in Germany have a saying for it: you can't ride two horses at the same time."

The kitchen stank of fish. Out in the yard, Emma saw nothing but mud and fir trees. No Vermont meadows, no view, just drizzle and fog shrouding the pond. She'd been getting to like the look of North Falls, but today it felt alien again.

157

"I can't stay here," she said.

Dee gave her a curious look, then shrugged. "Well, then, that's that," she said. "These have to process close to an hour over a hot fire. Thirty-eight fish is nine batches and some over. Cooker holds eight pints."

Arthur stood on the ridge above Hal's mill. The day was foggy and drizzling, but he barely noticed. His attention was focused on Hal's rifle in his hand. He slid off the safety and tried sighting, wanting to get the feel of it. It was an old-fashioned single shot, which was all right with him. Killing didn't take long, he figured, and one shot would have to do. Cain slew Abel. Three words, one sentence. He slipped the safety back on.

Hal had told him he'd find deer over north of the ranch. Arthur planned to circle on the ridge top and then drop down to the glades where they fed. He was walking a deer trail now, making good time. Rutting season was coming, they were active at dawn and dusk, hidden sleeping during the day. He'd heard the males snorting in the evening, loud honks like old men who pinched one nostril shut with a finger and blew out the other on the ground. The trail had plenty of fresh droppings. If he was any kind of man, it shouldn't be too hard, as least not for lack of a target. If.

He'd got it in his head that he wanted to shoot the deer that had jumped his fence last spring and eaten ten rows of peas down to nothing, then jumped back slick as lightning. Could hardly tell the peas had been there, the ground had been left that bare. Sharp, clear tracks had been pressed into the dirt like a seal into paper. Sharp little cloven hoofs. He'd had to replant, add brush to the fence, tie shiny can lids to the brush, sprinkle blood on the ground. That was the deer he wanted, or one of his kin would do, one from the local herd that plagued his place. Not a stranger. Family. Revenge was a dish to be eaten cold and he was about to get some revenge if it took all day. The feeling of it, or rather the lack of feeling, gave him a grim pleasure. He'd been feeling too much lately, mostly things that gave him pain. Getting this deer would take all of his attention so he wouldn't be able to feel the hurt of the rest.

But he felt it anyway. She didn't like his lovemaking, it came

158

down to that. She had been, perhaps still was, in love with somebody else. She had covered it over, hidden it from him till it was too late and he'd been trapped by caring about her. She was unruly and demanding and not at all like her sad and lovely poem. He had realized that after she'd waded the stream in her bare feet rather than follow him across it, but still he'd thought that in the matter of bed she'd know how to behave, know that there, at least, a man had to have things his own way. He'd been such a fool as ever was. Marry in haste, repent in leisure.

It was good to pull cold air into his lungs, to be out of the cabin, to stop mewling and act. He'd argued the matter in his mind too many times and he was sick of looking at his own mistakes, examining his priggish speech about courage and honesty, hearing her childish one about love. Both were nonsense. He wanted to kill the deer that had been disrupting his life. That was all. Though he'd seen how Hal admired Emma, played the gallant, pushed to get a rise out of Arthur. Hal thought he wanted her? Fine—let him have her. They could both go off to Seattle and good riddance. He'd go and see Elva maybe—ha! Elva had not one speck of loyalty, would run off with the first drummer to show up in town with a case full of painted feathers. He'd thought, from her poem, her picture, her letters, and the courting, that Emma was the girl for him and would be true. He was wrong.

When he came upon the animal, he realized it must have been there all along but he had been too preoccupied to spot it. Luckily the wind was in his favor and painful thoughts hadn't made him noisy in the woods—the critter was unalarmed. Horn buds, a young buck, alone and grazing. Probably hadn't won his own females yet, but was too mature to stay close around the herd. A loner and an outcast, like himself. A failure. It looked too young to be the one that had jumped his fence. Or maybe it could have been. He'd prevent its future jumps, or maybe jumping wasn't the issue; he didn't much care. For once he was not going to be overnice about reason and logic. Right or wrong, for once he was just going to do it. He would come out of the woods with game, not empty-handed like an asthmatic boy. He lifted the rifle. Took off the safety slow and quiet. Sighted at the liquid eye, which was like the Odd Fellows' single eye of God.

Then picked the bigger target where he knew the heart to be. Counted to ten and fired.

The noise was shocking and the gun kicked his shoulder so he didn't know if his aim had held steady or not. There was a crashing in the undergrowth, and when he entered the clearing, blood dripped from some twigs. He felt his own heart beat faster—he'd hit it, at least, good and proper. Because of the trail of blood, the tracking was short and easy. Thirty yards away the deer sagged to the ground and Arthur watched as the blood came in gushes, matching the pounding of his own heart. He felt like a murderer. His bullet had gone right through the neck, must have hit an artery, a lucky shot. The breathing turned ragged and the eye went glassy. His father had just gone upstairs for a nap and never woke up.

The deer lay on its side, 130 pounds, maybe. Coarse, dull hair, smooth flank bumped by a couple of ticks, dainty ankles thinner than a hoe handle. Arthur felt he was spying, as he had felt about Emma sleeping when she had first moved into his bed. A person had to be respectful looking at the dead, wish them well, for death could be catching. He reached to touch the deer—it was still warm. I did this, he thought, and was sorry. Then he thought—I could do it again if I had to. Kill an enemy, bring home meat to Em and our children. I hope I never have to do it again.

He'd take the deer down to Hal's to hang in the lumberyard, where there were hooks set in the shed rafters and a dog to keep off bears. First he had to dress it. Then tie it with the rope he'd brought and drag it out of the woods. He couldn't believe he'd finally done it after having avoided it all these years. Somber and awed, he sat on a rock by the body. It wasn't time to start gutting it yet. After a while it would be time.

I did this, he thought again, and was amazed. He wanted to tell someone about it, about how strange it was, about the picture of himself he'd brought to the woods as inadequate and different, and the knowledge he was taking away: he was just like other men, no better, no worse. What a discovery. He wanted to tell his father and Hal how it was, and he wanted a woman . . . not to know how it was, for that was impossible, but to know he'd done it.

"Dear Emma," he wrote in his head and then caught himself up. That Emma didn't exist any more, that perfect woman, virginal, adoring, attentive, biddable, unspoiled. If he was going to tell about it, he'd have to tell the Emma in his house. Who'd met her lover in the lanes and under the hedgerows in defiance of her father. Who worked hard and hung her dress on a peg to please him, but who wasn't about to let him get away with anything. On the way to the church to be married, she'd argued with him about the amount of time the Wright brothers actually kept their plane in the air. He'd said more than a minute; she'd said less. When they'd looked it up later, she'd been right. "Right about the Wright brothers," she'd said, and laughed, tickled with her pun, enjoying that she'd bested him. That Emma.

XXI

WHEN THE last jar went into the cooker, Emma thought Dee might sit down for a minute, put her feet up, and rest. That was what Emma wanted to do. She'd never canned meat before, only fruit and vegetables that took an open kettle, just a bath of boiling water. Being in the kitchen with a pressure cooker was exhausting—watching the steam gauge, stoking the fire, lifting the hot, slippery jars in and out, worrying that the whole cooker might explode. She felt fishy and wilted. What faced her at Arthur's was telling him of her decision to return home. She had to rest a few minutes first, compose herself.

Instead, Dee got out a big bowl of dough and started to roll out doughnuts.

"We're fresh out," she said to Emma, "and Mr. Brown doesn't feel at home in the world if the doughnut jar's empty." Her cutter flashed into the flour crock, into the dough, into the crock again. By the time she'd got four dozen stacked, the lard was boiling. The first ones dropped in to fry released the scent of nutmeg. Molly and Jane pulled open the hatch to the loft and peeked through.

"I smell doughnuts!" Molly yelled, rushing to turn herself around and climb down the steep rough steps. In her eagerness, she missed her footing and slid most of the way, limp as laundry. An adult would try to break the fall, catch hold, Emma thought, but children just let it happen to them. Molly's chin and knee knobs banged on every step and the sound of those thumps made Emma's bowels quake.

Molly landed and howled. Dee turned to assess her injuries.

162

Jane scrambled down the ladder and lunged at her mother's knees, throwing Dee back so her elbow whacked the pot of boiling lard. It tipped, righted itself precariously, sending a wave of hot fat up over the side where it splashed Jane on the arm and shoulder.

"Oh, my land," said Dee.

Molly cried, and Jane screamed, her baby face turned ancient in an instant. Emma remembered: a child's burned tongue and snow. The train station in White River Junction and Laura's face contorted. She scooped Jane up and ran with her in her arms to the pond. Wading into the icy water up to her waist, she managed to submerge Jane's arm and shoulder and to keep the rest of her somewhat dry.

"Lie still, lie still," she said to the terrified child, struggling to get down. "I've got you. I won't drop you. It'll feel better in the water."

The pond was fed by springs and snow on the mountains as well as by Smollett Creek. It made Emma's feet hurt, then ache, then go numb.

"Does that help?"

Jane nodded, lying quiet at last.

"You're being very good. You're a wonderful brave girl."

Though Emma's legs were losing all feeling, the weight of the child in her arms was a comfort to her. It made her know how much she'd missed Arthur's touch, not lovemaking, but the simple pleasure of body next to body, of skin next to skin. She remembered reading that skin was the largest organ people had and their chief interpreter of the world. She hoped Jane's skin wasn't too badly hurt.

She lifted Jane from the water, to take a look. "Are you six?" she asked, hoping to distract her from her pain during this examination.

"Going on seven in June."

"Do you know you're already in your seventh year?"

"Naw," said Jane, in disbelief.

Gently Emma peeled back Jane's cuff and floppy sleeve. There were bright red patches on the small, smooth limb and streaks of tiny blisters. "That's because you lived a whole year

163

before you had your first birthday. When people are born, they start at zero."

Exposed to air, the burn began to sting again and Jane's eyes filled with tears. "More water," she said, and leaned herself back into the pond. Emma saw her face relax as the icy cold did its work.

"So at your birthday, you'll be starting on your *eighth* year."

Emma feared this talk of birthday counting might be beyond the child, but she could see Jane listening hard, trying to take it in—and forgetting her injury.

"Eight's as old as Molly," Jane said, pleased with the idea of closing the gap between herself and her sister.

"How is she?" Dee called anxiously from the edge of the pond.

"Not too bad," Emma called, over her shoulder. "I'll bring her in in a minute. Get a dishpan full of this water ready. She doesn't hurt as much if her arm's wet and cold."

In the house they removed Jane's dress and pinafore. The cap of her shoulder was ballooned into a fiery puff, like a scarlet mushroom. Her arm was less severely burned. The child screamed as they got the cloth off her, quieted when the cold water treatment resumed. Dee, nursing Frieda, prepared whiskey for Jane, cut with water and sweetened. Molly, with her bruised knees, was allowed a spoonful, too.

Emma, sodden, started to shiver. "I'll be going back now," she told Dee, accepting her thanks but refusing an offer of dry clothes. She'd be gone for good Monday. She didn't want the complication of a borrowed dress. She kissed both of the little girls.

"We never got to play," Molly said.

Such little scorekeepers children were. It was on the tip of Emma's tongue to say, "We will another day soon," but she thought of Arthur and lying. "I know," she said. "I'm sorry."

She hurried along the logging road till she felt less numb, her shoes squishing juicily, her soaked skirts slapping at her ankles. She recalled the heft of Jane lying in her arms. She remembered Pa carrying Anne at bedtime when Anne was small. Anne had simply held out her arms and said, "I want to be *up,*" and up she went, into Pa's arms, and up the stairs. Emma had been filled with envy. "Carry me, too, Pa," she'd said, but Pa had said, "Got my hands full, Emma. Besides, you're my big girl." Her disappointment at not being carried had not been cancelled by being called "big." Who wanted to be big? She had wanted to be tiny and nestle in Pa's arms, or under his shirt, or inside his body, like a chick inside an eggshell.

In the rhythm of walking, tired and cold now after the rush to help with Jane, she half remembered, half dreamed that he had carried her, before Anne was born. Of course he had. He had carried her down to the creek to admire the cowslips, over to the neighbors' barn to see the new piglets, up to bed, just as he had carried Anne. She could recall the safety and warmth of it, the rocking motion of his legs, the thump of his heart as her ear lay pressed against his chest. Now that heart beat weakly, its steady pulse broken. "Go and be damned to you." Her own heart beat weakly. She was tired and cold, very cold.

Her step slowed. The sun had set while she was lost in thought. An icy wind had picked up and was cutting right through her wet clothes. She still had a ways to go before she reached the cabin. Her teeth chattered. She shivered uncontrollably.

The cabin was dark when she got there and the fire had gone out. Her mind, not thinking well at all, did not register that a wire basket of eggs and a pint tin can of milk sat on the table—Martin had done the chores and gone. She sat in the dark by the unlighted stove, not seeing her surroundings, trembling all over but no longer aware of being cold. Ordinarily she would have thought—I should clear away my breakfast things, Arthur likes a tidy house. It did not occur to her that she should get out of her wet dress, build a fire, drink something hot. Her mind ceased to function just as her body had. She didn't think, I could die of being so cold; I could lose consciousness and it wouldn't take long after that. She didn't think at all.

The numbness of the room deepened, lengthened. Time passed, a little, a lot. . . . She was so far gone she didn't hear the door swing open or footsteps. Someone struck a match, lighted a lamp, started a fire. Someone strong stood her up, which she could not do alone, stripped off her muddy clothes, wrapped her in a blanket. Pried open her jaw and poured hot

165

liquid into her mouth. Stroked her throat to get her to swallow. Made her walk up and down, though she didn't want to, she sagged at the knees, she just wanted to sink away into nothingness. Made her drink again. Said, "That's good, take some more." Made her walk.

Finally she was allowed to sit next to the fire in the blanket. Someone handed her a bowl of the hot liquid, folded her numb paws around it. When the heat seeped through to her fingers, they hurt.

"Ouch," she said.

"Aah!" said a voice like Arthur's, "keep drinking," and she drank and finally could taste the liquid—hot coffee and whiskey. It was Arthur lifting her feet, one at a time, and plunking them like a couple of bricks into a basin of hot water where her toes began to sting and prickle back to life.

"Hello, Arthur," she said. *Hél lo Aáh tha.*

"Well, Em. Are you back from the dead, then?" He smiled. She hadn't seen the wink of those overlapped side teeth, like sunlight dancing, in days. She basked in its warmth. Her body ached as though every muscle had been clenched up hard for hours.

"I hurt all over."

"That's a good sign that you're alive."

"Is it still today?" It seemed that years might have gone by.

"Just barely."

She remembered being at Dee's. "Jane," she said. "The hot lard spilled."

"I know all about it. Stopped by the Browns' on my way home. You did just the right thing for Jane—she's fine. But you were almost over the edge when I got here. At first I thought you were only asleep, but then, when I couldn't wake you . . ." He broke off when his voice began to quaver. He came to her chair, leaned down, and put his arms around her, hugging her so hard she could scarcely breathe.

"Thank you for bringing me back," she whispered into the side of his neck.

"I wasn't going to let you go, Em," he said, loosening his grip.

She remembered that she had been planning to go—back to

Vermont. "I've had a letter from Warwick," she told him. "On the table. You can read it."

He did, holding it to the lamp. "I'm sorry. He was displeased with you for coming here. It must be hard to know he's ill."

Ever since her bitter disappointment, when Arthur had failed to meet her train and she had almost broken down, she had vowed never to cry in front of him, only those few tears onto his horse's neck. Not from shame when she had belched into his mouth, not from pain when he first made love to her, not from angry hurt when he shut her out because of Paul. But now she wept, too weak to stop herself, though she was sure he would hate her for it. "Crying won't help," Ma had said when Emma fell out of the apple tree and skinned her knees. One of Aunt Josephine's maxims was that "a man scorns to see a woman cry." Even Clothilde, who cried when Tom dragged a dead sparrow into the house and who wallowed in sentiment on Memorial Day, liked to reiterate sadly, "Laugh and the world laughs with you; weep, and you weep alone." But Emma couldn't stop herself and she cried, not sweet and gentle tears, but loud, ugly, wracking ones.

Arthur came to her and put his hands on her hair. She circled her arms around his thighs, leaned her head against his belly. She wept for her buck teeth, losing Paul, being damned by Pa, wanting to love and be loved by Arthur, and having ruined that, too. She wept because Pa was going to die. She felt Arthur's hand stroking her hair.

"What do you think I should do?" she asked. She heard his belly gurgle. Her nose was running onto his shirt, but she didn't let go of him.

"What you want. I haven't been treating you right, Em, and I'm sorry. You'd be justified to go, I guess, considering, go and not return. I'm ready to let the past be the past. I hope you'll stay."

An enormous sob shook her. She hugged him hard, as though he were a tree trunk.

"Hey," he said.

She let him go, blew her nose, and wiped her face. "I was going to leave on Monday," she said. "Go down to Everett with

167

Hal and on from there. I'll find out how things are instead, send a wire. Anne's a letter writer. She'll tell me what's going on."

"Good," he said. "That's good. Now rest a bit, and I'll fix us a bite."

She stumbled to the bed. He put the quilt over her. She drew a deep breath and let it out in a shuddering sigh. She yawned, overcome with sleepiness, and pulled the quilt up over her ears. Some while later—minutes? an hour?—she woke, feeling fragile and newly made, to the hopeful smell of onions frying. Through the door she saw him—such an ordinary man to be her hero—holding a cold boiled potato in his left hand. He sliced off a piece with the jackknife in his right hand. He laid the slice in the pan, where it sizzled. He did that again, and again, each slice the same thickness, the same shape only smaller. The slices seemed miraculous to her, as beautiful as rose petals or snowflakes, and she continued watching, enchanted by potato slices. After a while came the hiss of meat hitting a hot pan. She got up, hungry, discovering that Arthur had unpinned her hair and dressed her in her flannel nightdress, a sweater, and a pair of his heavy woolen socks. She sat at the table where the breakfast dishes still stood, her face and teeth aglow, her hands in her lap. She felt as pampered as a guest.

"You bought fresh meat at Snows' today?" she said.

"It's venison. I got me a deer."

Arthur tried to announce it casually, as though he were saying no more than, "I bought a pound of nails," but joy leaked out all over his face and Emma saw it. She understood his need to damp his elation—get too happy and you tempt your family, friends, fate, and the gods to cut you down to size. But for her, at the moment, the old rules were off, left behind in New England along with the chastising climate and Puritan gloom. She wanted to celebrate his triumph, unrestrained.

"Say that again," she said.

"I got me a deer. Nice young buck. It's over to Hal's but for the liver. I'm cooking us a few slices, with a pile of onions."

Emma let out a whoop.

Arthur's face lit up the room. "Well, that's how I feel," he said. "You put it nicely."

"So you faced it down," she said proudly. "You went right out and did it."

"It wasn't so hard, once I'd made my mind up to it. It helped feeling desperate, as though I had to do *something* because things between us had come to such a pass."

"What were we fighting about?" she asked, knowing that they had been but truly forgetting the details.

"Everything," he said, and laughed. "Do you like your venison liver a little bit rare?"

"I do. And I like you even better, best of all. Let's start being married all over, as of now."

"Suits me right down to the ground," said Arthur. He served each of them a plate of food and a glass of whiskey and water. After they'd eaten, he took her hand and led her to the bed.

"Let's try this again," he said. "I can see I've got to learn how to court you, Emma Howe."

The bedroom was warm and lit by firelight. He took a long time undressing and admiring her, and this time was not shy about undressing himself. She found him strange and beautiful to look at. At first when he began to touch her, she felt like a swimmer treading water in the shallows, while Arthur called to her silently to join him in the river's central current. But before long, he pulled her with him to where the water was fast-moving and deep. Thought left her, awareness of herself as separate left her. Afterwards, holding him in her arms, she felt herself return from someplace quite far away. I am lying down in a green pasture, she thought. More bits of language drifted unbidden through her mind, expressions she'd known all her life that suddenly had the right fit, or more Bible phrases to which she gave, unashamed, her own pagan meanings. "Like a warm knife into butter." "Thy rod and thy staff they comfort me." "And they shall be one flesh."

XXII

THE MORNING of Mr. Parsons's funeral, Emma was down on her knees, working. June had come, warm and bright. All of a sudden, everything needed weeding, thinning, transplanting, and watering, at the very same time. The gardens were like children clamoring in chorus for attention: I'm hungry! I'm thirsty! Read me a story!

Watering! All of a sudden the North Falls sky, which she had thought of as a large, sodden sponge, had been transformed. Warm, blue, sunny days came weeks at a time, days that were miraculously dry. Arthur had a holding tank and gravity feed from the creek to the gardens, but still the hoses had to be shifted and the whole network of valves and pipes overseen. They were actually watering. Who would have thought?

Wearing a straw hat, a long-sleeved shirt, and a pair of Arthur's overalls, Emma worked her way methodically down the rows, pulling the spindly seedlings and leaving the stout. Radish, mustard, spinach, kale. The thinnings would go into a salad at dinner time, dressed with vinegar and sugar, after which it would be time to get cleaned up for Jason Parsons's funeral. Emma remembered shaking Mr. Parsons's hand, the day she saw Arthur's ranch for the first time. He had dropped dead of a heart attack, never sick a day in his life, a good way to go. He had been an important Odd Fellow, and as secretary, Arthur was to be a pall bearer. A Saturday and nice weather—Emma was actually looking forward to the outing. It was a good day for a funeral.

She liked having her hands in the black, rich soil, liked its

170

odor. When she was tempted to eat a pinch, she smiled to herself. That's the final sign, she thought—I really must be pregnant. The taste might be good, but not the texture—she contented herself with deep satisfying sniffs. When she got tired of crawling, she sat, hitching herself along, working neither fast nor slow. There was always something to attend to on the ranch, work to be done, but no need to rush. Tending the gardens was a turtle game of slow and steady, a long steady hike, not a sprint. Its pace matched that of the presence in her abdomen, which needed to be carried for a long time till it was ready to be born. She'd suspected, treasuring her secret, not wanting to tell Arthur till she was sure. It was a couple of months, and now she was certain. This yeasty day, when you could practically sit back on your heels and watch the seedlings burst out of the ground, would be a fine one for whispering her news to him, once the funeral was over.

She sang in her mind one of Pa's favorite songs: "If I had the wings of an angel, Over these prison walls would I fly. I'd fly to the arms of my darling, and there I would willingly die." Over and over, never getting tired of it, in fact, barely noticing that she was doing it. Was there more to it, a middle section, a second verse? She neither knew nor cared. She sang it again.

A shadow on the ground announced someone had come, a shadow too bulky to be Arthur's. She knew a lot about him now, private things that only she could know. When he was a boy, he'd wanted to play shortstop for the Red Sox. He buttered his bread to the crusts and cut it in triangles, bit off the points first. He was a moderate eater, had a sweet tooth, but didn't put on weight—his shadow would never be as big as the one she saw.

"Morning, Emma," Hal said. "I've come to say good-bye."

With the sun spang behind him, Hal was just a black silhouette to her. She scrambled up and brushed herself off, moved so she could see her husband's friend.

"Hello, Hal," she said. "Arthur's cleaning out the holding tank, you'll find him over there. Where're you going?"

"Seattle, this time to stay, Martha's oldest's going to run things from this end while I'll open the city branch of the business, figure a boy who steps on a rusty spike and lives to tell the tale has luck on his side and should do well. I've been dreaming about Seattle five years at least and now I'm going to do it, knew I'd see you and Art at the funeral but that's no place to be telling news, now is it?"

Seattle, she thought with a pang of envy—I never did get there. And Hal gone—we'll miss him, Arthur most of all. "He'll be in for dinner soon, I expect," she told Hal. "Stay and eat some with us so you can tell him your plans yourself. He'll be amazed, you know, and you'll be a loss to him. He'll want to hear."

"Perhaps I'll walk out and find him, I'm sorry to leave you both, Emma, you've been good friends to me, can't stay to dinner, though, lots to do, we leave tomorrow."

"Tomorrow—already? *We?*"

Hal blushed from the top of his beard to the top of his forehead. "Elva's found a place there, too, clerking in a ladies' dress shop, we're going down together, I guess you might say, it's just coincidence, of course, but it makes the trip more friendly, I told Bert and Dee I'd keep an eye on her in the city, she's young to be there on her own, you know what I mean, Emma, now don't look at me that way, there's nothing more to it than that, I swear."

Emma pressed her lips together to keep from smiling. "You and I never took our trip together, did we, Hal?"

"You canceled out on me, left me high and dry to go alone, you and Art come and see me, now, I'm expecting you, I'll show you the sights of Seattle yet, Emma, indeed I will." His enormous hands shook both of hers, stained with dirt.

"That would be nice," she said with another pang, knowing they would never go—she would never be able to pry Arthur loose from his ranch to visit the hated city. "Good luck to you, Hal."

Before the funeral, she and Arthur bathed in the creek, both of them with farmer's tans—brown hands and faces, brown V's at their throats, the rest of them white. Emma liked the look of Arthur's wedged shaped back, was still a little shocked at his buttocks when he did a surface dive, like two attached white bakery buns, something faintly indecent about them. The water was silky, the color of root beer. She swam to the center of the pool to rinse her hair, hesitated, then did a surface dive herself. Arthur was grinning at her when she came up.

"Do another."

"Get along with you."

When she waded out of the cold water, feeling pink and alive, he kissed her, rubbing his hands lightly over both her nipples.

"Not here," she said. She scooped up her sweaty clothes and darted back toward the cabin, wanting him to chase her. He grabbed his own clothes and followed laughing, at a run.

Afterwards in their best clothes they ate dinner and walked down to the funeral, where the scent of semen on them mingled with the scent of flowers for the dead.

While Arthur went to help carry the casket, Emma chose a seat on the right, in the middle. The fine day, and Mr. Parsons's position, had guaranteed a good turnout for the service. Already several pews were occupied. Martha Landis arrived, making one of her rare appearances in town, for she preferred staying with her brood at the mill. She sat with Emma. Elva, in flowered gingham, settled herself between Bert and Dee, playing the dutiful daughter. Annie Vogel was getting big in front, but she was there with Martin.

"Hello, Emma," Annie whispered from across the aisle. Her dress had the waist set high on the rib cage. Emma waved, noting the details of design.

The Snows were good friends of the Parsonses and took places at the front, Harry steering his pot belly like a small ship before him, Millie turning her head from side to side as though counting the house. No one was minding the store, but it didn't matter for the mail had gone and all potential customers would be in church.

There was a pause, for latecomers. The children's choir, among them Sonny Snow, Molly Brown, and at least three Landises, sang, "Lead, Kindly Light." Then Madge Parsons, massive as a bison in black silk, lumbered in from the left side of the altar on the arm of her beanpole son, Bill. At the same time, Amos Brill, ginger whiskers shining rather brightly for a funeral, appeared at the right. Another pause, and then the heavy tread of the pallbearers came down the aisle. The congregation

173

rose, turned toward the back, looking for the casket as they would have looked for the bride.

Arthur was wearing his seal of office and carrying one of the front corners. He looked handsome to Emma, solemn and dignified—manly. The whole procession was serious and careful, as they had to be since the heights of the bearers ranged from Arthur to Hal and they were trying to keep the casket more or less level. Slowly they walked forward; steadily they placed their burden on the raised platform waiting for it. Mr. Parsons, who looked so much like Pa that for a split second Emma's breath caught in her throat, was wearing his best suit and Odd Fellows seal. His hands were folded over a black Bible. He looked peaceful. The sight of him, as he lay in his coffin, brought tears to Emma's eyes. It was Ma, not Anne, who had written: "I am taking care of Pa. If I were you, I would not come. You have a new life now. The doctor thinks Pa has had a second smaller stroke for he scarcely knows anyone, and it's so far." Shutting her out? Letting her go?

Arthur joined her. She wanted to take his hand but refrained for he disapproved of public shows of feeling, another piece of private knowledge she had recently acquired by kissing him on the road in view of the store and having him pull away. Her feelings had been hurt. He'd had to explain.

The service moved on through eulogy, song, and prayer, till Arthur left her to help carry the casket out to the freshly dug grave. More prayers. The lowering of the wooden box into the black dirt. Madge, who up till now had been quiet and dry-eyed, let out a cry when Amos Brill handed her a clod to throw.

"He was the only one," she sobbed, "who knew me when I was young and slim." The clod, when she finally let it drop from her hand, thudded loud on the coffin lid as though the box were empty. Bill Parsons, narrow shouldered and alone beside his mother, threw his chunk of dirt, and then the other mourners, anxious to help, added theirs. Emma could see Pa in his chair at the Warwick kitchen table, silent, fading, partly in this world and partly in the next. Tears ached in her throat, but she held them back. She prayed for Pa, and for Mr. Parsons, and for all the graveside mourners, not asking for anything from God in

174

the sky but praying for their ability to bear life's unfairness and to tolerate—even be kind to—one another.

When the burial was over, and the short reception, and the good-byes said, she took Arthur's arm—linking arms was acceptable, though holding hands was not. She wanted to walk up the road and up the trail with him, feeling the slow rhythm of haunches, legs, and feet. She wanted to see his face when she told him her secret.

"Let's go home," she said, and the minute the words were out was aware of the change. It wasn't "Arthur's ranch" anymore. It had become her place.